Libby would never forget the intimacy she had felt in the presence of Jesus with Greg by her side. . . .

It would be so easy to take the little bit Greg was offering, even simple friendship, but Libby knew she would only be setting herself up for future heartbreak. She had to be strong.

"Well," Greg was saying, "I just thought it would be appropriate for us to go back and thank Jesus for answering our prayer in such a wonderful way."

Libby felt a chill run through her body. That was such an incredibly beautiful thought. If only she and Greg—but no, she must not let herself even dream of such an impossibility.

"I'm sorry, Greg. I can't come, but I'll thank Him right here from my home. And thank you so much for sharing with me this morning."

"Right. Well then, I'll be seeing you, Libby. Take care of yourself."

"Give my love to Patty, and to Danny too." *But most of all, to you, Greg. I wish I could tell you how I feel.* Libby replaced the receiver and wiped a tear from each eye.

MUNCY G. CHAPMAN has four children who magically became eight (with the addition of their spouses), and then was blessed with eleven grandchildren. All live in Florida. She says she is married to the most wonderful man in the world with whom she recently celebrated their golden wedding anniversary. Muncy likes to sew, cook, play the piano, and of course, write. She works with the children in her church, and also with the shut-ins as a "Caring Caller." She enjoys writing with her husband. He likes the research and she likes choosing the words.

Books by Muncy G. Chapman

HEARTSONG PRESENTS
HP266—What Love Remembers
HP319—Margaret's Quest
HP361—The Name Game

Condo Mania

Muncy G. Chapman

Heartsong Presents

Lovingly dedicated to my big brothers,
John Owen Gallagher
Charles William Gallagher

A note from the author:
I love to hear from my readers! You may correspond with me by writing: **Muncy G. Chapman**
Author Relations
PO Box 719
Uhrichsville, OH 44683

ISBN 1-58660-169-5

CONDO MANIA

Cover illustration by Kay Salem.

PRINTED IN THE U.S.A.

one

Libby Malone lowered the window of her white compact car and stretched to push her plastic card into the slot of the automatic gate lock. She allowed her motor to idle as she waited for the steel arm of the barricade to rise and admit her into the Blue Dolphin Condominiums, and from her rearview mirror, she watched it close behind her after she drove through.

She left her window down as she proceeded along the flower-laden double drive, allowing the wind to ruffle her long blond hair. Creeping along at the posted fifteen mile-per-hour speed limit, she drove past the big shimmering lake. Sunlight bounced off the red tile roofs that topped the elegant Spanish-styled condominiums sprinkled among the rolling hills on either side of the road. She braked to a complete stop to relinquish the right-of-way to a pair of stately sandhill cranes and watched them strut across the drive. The proud, graceful creatures exhibited no fear as they crossed in front of her, holding their red crowns high in the air. *This place is like one big beautiful garden,* she mused.

Libby followed the curving drive past her office in the administration building where she usually stopped first thing every morning. But today was no ordinary morning. Libby's stomach churned just thinking about it.

Proceeding at a snail's pace, Libby drove down the road toward the Blue Dolphin clubhouse, where residents were already beginning to congregate for the specially called Property Owners Association meeting. There was sure to be a crowd today with such a volatile issue at stake, and Libby was less than pleased to find herself right in the middle of the brewing controversy.

As assistant property manager, she had worked alongside Jake Wilkowski for the past two wonderful years, ever since finishing her property management course at the local junior college and passing her state test to become a licensed Community Association manager. She was grateful to Michael Phillips, owner of Four Star Property Managers, for hiring her with no hands-on experience and assigning her to the Blue Dolphin Condominiums.

"You're a lucky young lady," Michael had told her that day. "With Jake Wilkowski as your mentor, you'll be interning under the best in the industry." And in the ensuing two years, Libby never had reason to doubt that statement. Jake had taken her under his wings of experience and taught her every facet of successful condominium management, including practical things that were not covered in her college courses. And he had become the best friend she had ever known.

Jake's sudden death had left Libby with a deep personal loss that reached far beyond her job at Blue Dolphin.

She parked her car in front of the clubhouse and walked toward the double-door entrance.

"Good morning, Libby!" Residents making their way into the building greeted her by name, and she responded with more gaiety than she felt.

The meeting room was filled with folding chairs, and as residents and guests filed in to find their seats, Libby took her place beside Michael Phillips at the long table at the front of the room. The president of the Property Owners Association, along with the vice president, the secretary, and treasurer, all took seats at the table.

The tension in the room was almost palpable. There were neither jokes nor laughter, and even a stranger could have perceived the purpose of this meeting was a somber one.

President Selena Watson sat at the center of the table. A head of teased blond hair crowned the lines in her thin, severe face. The upward tilt of her chin gave her an air of superiority as she called the meeting to order.

After completing the routine opening procedures, Selena addressed the group. "I think all of you know why we have called this special emergency meeting today."

Rumbles and nods swept through the room, and all eyes were directed to the head table as Selena continued.

"There is no way to assess the loss to Blue Dolphin by the death of our on-site manager, Jake Wilkowski. I'm sure I speak for all of you when I say we will miss him in a most personal way. But today, we are here to discuss that loss in a more pragmatic way. Specifically, how is his death going to impact Blue Dolphin, and what are we planning to do about it? I am going to turn the microphone over to Mr. Phillips who represents Four Star Property Management Company to let you hear his suggestions. Mr. Phillips. . ."

Michael's impeccable grooming, along with his tall stature and silver-gray hair gave him an air of mature distinction. He adjusted his tie and cleared his throat as he stood to address the crowd. "Madam President, I want to assure you and all of the residents here at Blue Dolphin that we intend to continue as we have in the past, to provide you with the best possible care and management of your property. There will be no interruption in any of the services we currently provide. Of course, the question uppermost in your minds today is, just who will be your new on-site manager? You are fortunate to have Libby Malone already in place. As your assistant manager for the last two years, she is already familiar with every inch of your property. Most of you know her personally and respect her knowledge and integrity."

"Mis-ter Phillips," Selena interrupted in a voice loud enough to be heard even without benefit of a microphone. "I hope you are not suggesting that Miss Malone will now be the person responsible for this entire complex."

Soft murmurs from the audience swelled as though the volume button of a remote control had suddenly been pushed, and Selena rapped her gavel to restore order. Libby's cheeks burned as she listened to Selena's clipped words.

"With all due respect to the very charming Miss Malone, I agree she is completely adequate as an *assistant* to the manager." She aimed a plastic smile in Libby's direction. "But with four hundred units in this association, I believe we deserve someone with a proven track record to assume full charge."

Michael spoke into his microphone, choosing his words with great care. "Madam President, I only meant to point out that Miss Malone's presence would allow uninterrupted service until such time as we are able to make a final decision on your new on-site manager. However, I would like to further point out that in view of her past performance, she might be a logical candidate for the position."

Hands shot up all over the room, and the president recognized them one by one. Libby heard residents rising to her defense, telling of the many ways in which she had helped them, and testifying to her character and attitude. These comments were shouted down by dissenting voices pointing out that she was quite young, and that her brief two-year tenure might not have provided adequate experience for such a large responsibility. Someone even dared to declare that she was a woman who would be trying to perform a man's work.

Tempers flared and words flew back and forth across the room like enemy missiles. At last, Selena pounded her gavel. *"Order!"* she screamed. "I would like to hear a motion that we table this discussion until we have had time to explore our options with cool heads."

The motion came quickly and was promptly seconded. As a result of the ensuing discussion, the board decided that Libby Malone would be allowed to serve as interim on-site manager until the appointment of a permanent manager. Selena took one last jab at Libby before she officially adjourned the meeting. "My friends, time is of the essence in this matter. Irreparable damage can occur rapidly from mismanagement, and to insure this does not happen to our beautiful Blue Dolphin properties, I will be meeting with Mr. Phillips immediately to resolve this situation." She rapped her gavel and firmly declared the meeting to be adjourned.

Libby pushed her chair back from the table and rose to her feet on knees that felt like Jell-O. She was disappointed that in the two years she had spent working among the people of Blue Dolphin, she had not been able to convince Selena and some of the others of her competency. What more had they expected of her? Should she speak to Selena and try to alleviate some of her concerns? But what could she possibly say now that would make a whit of difference? It seemed clear that Ms. Watson had firmly made up her mind, and nothing was going to sway it.

Before Libby had time to formulate her thoughts, a commotion erupted in the far back corner that quickly converted the already noisy room into complete pandemonium.

Libby stood on her tiptoes trying to see the cause of it all. What she saw at the back of the room caused her to freeze in shock. A frail elderly woman was precariously standing on a folding chair, shrilling, "Get that thing away from me!"

A fall from the chair could be disastrous for anyone, but particularly for someone of that age! Libby swallowed the lump of terror lodged in her throat and elbowed her way through the crowd.

A tall husky man, his face red with anger, had a firm grip on the arms of a small howling boy, as he held him high in the air.

Facing the angry man was a dark-haired man whose rock-hard physique made up for his slightly smaller stature. His face was equally reddened from anger as he shouted in the other man's face, "Put that boy down. Take your hands off him *this instant!*"

Libby recognized them all. The lady on the chair was Mrs. Frierson, whose bent to hysteria was reluctantly accepted by all who knew her. What had upset her this time? Libby continued to push her way through the crowd and prayed she could get to Mrs. Frierson in time to prevent a fall that might result in a broken hip or worse.

The young boy was still held aloft by the hands of Mr. Gabbard, the man who earlier had voiced his unfavorable opinion of females in management positions—especially young ones. Lon Gabbard had strong opinions about everything—usually negative opinions—which he was never reluctant to share with anyone who would pause to listen to him.

And the man who had risen to the defense of the boy, his son, was Blue Dolphin's newest resident, Greg Cunningham.

As Libby reached the scene of the melee, she caught a glimpse of Selena striding toward the front door, a determined look on her stern, narrow face. Selena paused and turned, obviously to see how Libby would handle this volatile situation.

By the time Libby reached the back of the room, Lon Gabbard had already lowered the boy to the floor and helped Mrs. Frierson down from her chair.

"What is it, Mrs. Frierson? What happened?" Libby asked.

The elderly lady appeared to be gasping for her last breath. "That—that—boy! He has a *frog* in his jacket! Get that thing out of here!"

For the life of her, Libby could not maintain a solemn expression. Her lips curved upward, but she turned to the child and said, "Is that true, Danny? Do you have a frog in your jacket?" It was hard to sound stern whenever she looked at Danny's mischievous face. Tousled red hair hung over his freckled forehead as he nodded sheepishly. "Yes'm, but I didn't mean to let him get out, honest. I'll take him home with me right now."

"Well, Danny, I think it might be nice if you apologized to Mrs. Frierson. You frightened her, and besides, you know we have a rule against animals in the clubhouse. In fact, pets are not allowed in Blue Dolphin at all."

Seeing the crestfallen look on his impish face, Libby put a hand on his shoulder to let him know they were still friends.

"I'm sorry, Ma'am," Danny muttered, and pressed his small frame against his father. Mrs. Frierson allowed two men to escort her toward the front door, mopping her forehead with her lace-edged handkerchief and muttering all the way.

Libby turned her attention to Danny's father. In a face bronzed by the sun, Greg Cunningham had the bluest eyes she had ever seen. Libby found it hard to look into them and keep her mind on the stern reprimand he deserved for allowing his seven-year-old son to disrupt the meeting.

"I'm sorry too, Miss Malone. I'm afraid I lost my cool when Lon Gabbard grabbed hold of my son. But this matter was not his to handle. I'll deal with Danny myself when we get home, and I'll see this doesn't happen again."

"I realize you're new here, Mr. Cunningham, but we'll have to come to an understanding about the rules and regulations here at Blue Dolphin. But this is neither a good place nor a good time to discuss it. Could you call my office for an appointment so we can sit down together and I can review the bylaws with you?"

"I'll look forward to that," he said, giving her a playful wink.

Although Libby found his dimpled smile disarming, she was less than pleased with his casual brush-off of what she considered a potential problem—a problem she'd have to deal with before it was allowed to develop any further. This was precisely the sort of thing that could help or hinder her in achieving her goal of property manager.

"Perhaps tomorrow then," she suggested. "And I'd like Danny to be there too. Just call the secretary for an appointment." Without waiting for his answer, Libby turned on her heels and walked away.

By now the clubhouse was almost empty. Libby went out through the front door in time to see Selena drive off in her red convertible. That woman had never liked her, and for the life of her, Libby could not figure why. She had asked Jake about it once, and he had brushed the matter aside like a fly that had lit on his shirtsleeve. "Just do your job to the best of your ability, put your trust in God, and the rest will take care of itself."

Libby had tried to follow that advice, but she had continued to feel a wall of animosity separating her from Selena whenever their paths crossed. And it looked as though their paths would be crossing more and more, now that Libby was to be the interim manager of the complex. She was certain the interim would be a very short one if Selena Watson had her way.

She unlocked her car door and slid into the front seat, but not before Michael Phillips approached and waved to her. She lowered her window and he leaned into the car. "Look, Libby, I'm sorry about all the fracas, but we do need to talk. Are you on your way back to the office now?"

"Yes, of course. I'd planned on going over some bills. I'll be right up."

&

The administration building was located just inside the front gate. A secretary sat at a desk in the reception area to greet and direct office traffic. Jake's office had claimed the back half of the small building; Libby's office was a small cubicle on the right.

Michael was already waiting for her when she walked in the door. Libby greeted the secretary before she turned her attention to her employer. "That was quite a meeting this morning, wasn't it?"

"Yes, quite," Michael agreed noncommittally before he opened the door to Jake's office. "Let's talk in here where we won't be interrupted." As soon as the door was closed behind them, he finished his comment by saying, "You might as well move your things in here, Libby. It will be your office, at least for now."

Michael sat at Jake's big desk, and Libby positioned herself across from him. She adjusted her skirt and waited for him to begin the discussion.

Michael shifted uncomfortably in his chair. "Libby, you know I'd like to see you as the on-site manager here. I know you're as capable as anyone else—more so, in fact."

"But. . . ," Libby prompted, trying to put him at ease. She knew what a difficult spot this must be for him.

"I'll be meeting with the board of directors later this week, and I'll give you the highest recommendation I can, because you truly deserve it, Libby. But you know the final decision will rest with the board. Four Star property managers can't risk losing this account by being arbitrary. Blue Dolphin is one of our largest clients."

"I know that, Michael. But I also know I can be an efficient manager if they'll give me the chance. What can I do to convince them I can handle the job?"

"Just what you've been doing—tending to business and keeping your pleasant disposition in place. I know it isn't easy sometimes, like this morning. And that episode with the little Cunningham boy is just the sort of thing Selena Watson is watching for, just waiting for you to make a mistake that she can use against you."

"That was an unfortunate event," Libby admitted. "I've asked Mr. Cunningham to come in so I can go over the condominium rules with him. And I've asked him to bring his son along so I can talk to him too."

"Refresh my memory, Libby. Just how did we allow them to move into Blue Dolphin in the first place? I've been questioned about this by several of the residents who are quick to remind me that this community is supposed to be restricted to residents fifty-five years of age or older."

There was a logical explanation, and Libby hastened to offer it. "That's true, and we always interview prospective residents before they close on their new property. But technically speaking, Greg Cunningham and his son are not residents—they are guests of his mother. The owner, Lenore Cunningham, lives in the unit six months of the year, but she goes up north to Michigan every summer as soon as the weather gets hot. She was still occupying the unit when her son and grandson arrived, but she left a few days later. I've researched the bylaws on that point and found nothing that says the owner has to remain in residence during the entire time she has guests. The only rule I dug up was one that limits visits by children to a maximum of ninety consecutive days during a calendar year, but Greg and his son have only been here for a few weeks."

"Well, why would they want to stay on visiting his mother if she has already gone north? There aren't any other children around here for the youngster to play with, and we don't even have any playground equipment to make this place attractive to families with young children."

Libby's mouth curved upward in a brief smile. "Perhaps that's the very reason why Danny is always getting into mischief!" The smile lasted but an instant, then vanished as quickly as it had appeared. This whole matter could turn into an explosive situation for her. She could not afford to make light of it. "I'll talk to them tomorrow to make sure they both understand we can't tolerate any more rule infractions. Aside from the Cunningham situation, do you have any suggestions that might help my cause here at Blue Dolphin? Because I really want this position, Michael."

"Libby, you know the board of directors has the final word on this. I plan to meet with Selena and the rest of the board to discuss it, and I'll certainly try to put in a good word for you. Beyond that, my hands are tied. That's all I can do."

Michael started to rise, then reclaimed his chair to present another point. "Where are you meeting the Cunninghams, Libby? Here in your office?"

"Why, yes, that's what I'd planned. Is there a problem with that?"

"No, on the contrary, that's where you *should* meet, to avoid any. . .um. . .confusion."

"I don't understand, Michael. What are you getting at?"

"Just being supercautious for your benefit, Libby. You know how tongues can wag, especially among people who don't have enough to occupy their time. You're an attractive young lady, and Mr. Cunningham is. . .well. . .he's also young, and. . ."

Libby straightened her spine and squared her shoulders. "Surely you're not suggesting—"

"I'm not suggesting anything. Now, simmer down and don't take offense, Libby." Michael stood and placed both hands on the desk, leaning forward to meet her eyes. "Remember, I want to help you. I'm just reminding you of the company policy that strictly forbids staff fraternizing with the residents. It can lead to accusations of favoritism or worse, and I want to spare you any unwarranted criticism. And I'm sure you know Selena Watson's unit is situated just across the courtyard from the Cunningham condo."

A rosy flush colored Libby's face. "I'm aware of the Four Star policy, Michael. I'm surprised you thought I needed a reminder."

"Libby, I'm only trying to give you every advantage." He straightened and edged toward the door. "I'm sorry to leave all this mess in your hands, but I have another meeting with the manager of Coral Sands Condominiums across town. I know you'll handle everything here with your usual competence."

Libby stood and extended her hand. "Forgive me if I seemed a little touchy. This has been a stressful morning. I really appreciate your help, and I'll do my best to warrant your trust."

When Michael left the room, Libby sat down again at the big desk that was now hers. She buried her face in her hands. As she closed her eyes to hold back the hot tears that pressed against her lids, she could almost feel the presence of her mentor who had sat in this very chair, guiding her through every possible problem. "Oh, Jake, how I'm going to miss you! Working with you was so special. You always knew just how to handle difficult situations. I'd have been content to work as your assistant for as long as you wanted me, but now that you're gone, I'm not willing to stand back and let someone else move into your place. I know I can do this job as well or better than anyone else, because I've had the best teacher in the world. But I sure could use some of your great advice right now!"

Without raising her face, she sat in meditation with only the clock on the wall daring to intrude on her silence. Then as clear as though he were in the room with her, she began to hear Jake's words echoing through her mind. *Just do your job to the best of your ability, put your trust in God, and the rest will take care of itself.*

A feeling of warmth swept over her like a soft autumn breeze, filling her heart with renewed hope and energy. Libby shook the hair from her face and raised her eyes, ready to begin the difficult task that had been set before her.

æ

Michael Phillips drove out the gate of Blue Dolphin with a heavy heart. He had read the desperation in Libby Malone's soft brown eyes and hoped he was wrong in what he guessed the outcome of this dilemma would be. She was a sweet kid, and he had to admit she knew the condo business better than some of his older, more experienced managers on staff at Four Star Property Managers.

He'd been placing property managers for over twenty-five years. Today was not the first time he had encountered this kind of problem among condominium residents. In fact, he saw it all too often. Sometimes it was hard for members of the senior generation to relinquish their claim to wisdom and experience to people young enough to be their grandchildren.

Thankfully, those few shortsighted, inflexible individuals did not constitute the majority in this peaceful community, but they did represent a very vocal and powerful minority. Selena Watson was a prime example. He was certain Selena would use her power of persuasion to try to oust Libby Malone, and he would end up having to replace Jake Wilkowski with someone else from his staff. A male, of course. It was unfortunate, but that's the way the condominium game was played.

He put Blue Dolphin out of his mind and turned his thoughts to Coral Sands, and the meeting he had scheduled next on his agenda. He glanced at his Rolex. He'd have to move right along if he expected to arrive on time.

two

"Hurry up, Danny. You'll make us late for the meeting at the Blue Dolphin office, and we already have enough black marks on our record there. You want us to get thrown out of this place?"

"I wouldn't mind one little bit," Danny sulked, looking up from the plastic dinosaurs he was arranging in a line on the pale plush carpet. "I hate it here. There's nothin' for me to do, and nobody here likes me, anyway."

"Well, Buddy, I can find plenty for you to do when we get back. For starters, you could pick up your dirty clothes off the bathroom floor." Seeing Danny's downcast eyes, Greg realized his usually jovial son was in no mood for teasing today.

Ever since the death of his wife four years ago, Greg had tried his best to be both father and mother to Danny, but at times like this, he felt grossly inadequate. "Look, Buddy, we just have to tough it out here for a couple of months until our new house is finished. Then things are going to be different for us."

"Yeah, they'll be different all right! A lot of things!" There was no joy in Danny's voice as he struggled to tie the laces of his new sneakers. "I may just stay on here with Grandma when she gets back."

That response caught Greg by surprise. He'd have thought staying on at Blue Dolphin would have about as much appeal for Danny as eating broccoli for lunch every day. "That's not one of your options, Son. Besides, what would I do without my best buddy?"

"You'd do fine," Danny growled. "I know you're thinkin' about marryin' Tiffany, and I'm sure not livin' in the same house with her."

18

"Now, just simmer down, Danny. Nobody has said anything about getting married to anybody. Where did you get an idea like that?"

"Well, that's the way it usually happens on television. And why is she so sappy over our new house? She walks through it like she owns the place, tellin' you to put a mirror here and a closet there. What business is it of hers, if she's not even gonna live there?"

"Nothing's been decided yet, Danny. Besides, every time you have to wash the dishes, you tell me I should find you a new mother. I thought you'd been hounding me to find a wife!"

"Humph! Well, I sure wouldn't want to have anybody like Tiffany for my mom! I'd never get to—"

"Come on, Buddy. It's time to go."

❧

Libby added her signature to the last check in the pile Lorraine had stacked on her desk. She rubbed her tired eyes and heaved a sigh. The day had started badly for her early this morning, when the irrigation system had malfunctioned and unexpectedly doused some early walkers. She'd spent an hour getting the clock on the pump adjusted, and another hour cooling the tempers of the angry walkers. And she certainly wasn't looking forward to this visit from the two Cunninghams.

In spite of the fact that Danny was always into some kind of mischief, she felt a strong attraction to the little guy. He seemed awfully sweet, and it wasn't his fault he was living in a condominium community that did not provide for children. And where was his mother? Perhaps Danny's problems stemmed from a lack of individual attention, although in all fairness, the father did appear to be very dedicated to the care of his son. She seldom saw one without the other.

Libby's thoughts were interrupted by the buzzer on her intercom. She picked up the receiver and brought her mind back to her work. "Yes?"

"The Cunninghams are here to see you."

"Thanks, Lorraine. Could you bring them in? See if Danny would like a can of root beer from the fridge. I'm going to have to scold him a little, but I want him to realize we're his friends."

Moments later, her office door swung open and Greg Cunningham walked in, followed closely by his son. Danny was clutching an unopened can of root beer, and he was eyeing Libby with a guarded expression.

Libby smiled and tried to put him at ease. "Please sit down." She indicated the two chairs across from her desk.

"I'm not exactly sure why we're here, Miss Malone, but—"

"Please, Mr. Cunningham, everyone here just calls me Libby."

"Okay, Libby. And I'm Greg." His smile revealed a pronounced dimple in each cheek, and the lock of dark hair that fell over his forehead gave him a winsome, schoolboy look. And oh, those eyes!

Libby shuffled the papers on her desk and fastened her focus on the pages. How ridiculous that she should be charmed by this man who had brought nothing but trouble into her already upside-down world. She picked up her pen and gave the outward appearance of scanning the text.

"What I want to do, Mr. Cunning—um, Greg,—is go over the condominium bylaws and make sure you understand the rules."

"I understand there are quite a lot of them, and I must admit, some of them seem pretty silly to me."

Just as Libby had feared, her guest was less than happy to be here, and was not likely to be cooperative unless strongly persuaded to be so. "That may be true. In fact, I've questioned some of them myself from time to time. Yet the people who live here are the ones who've decided what they want, and as their manager—" Libby choked on the title—"as their. . .um, *interim* manager, it is my responsibility to see that their rules are carried out."

Greg folded his arms across his chest in a classic stubborn, unyielding pose. "Okay, so no frogs in the clubhouse. What else?"

Libby tried to ignore the sarcasm in his voice. "Let's just run down the page and I'll try to point out the ones that might give you some concern."

Danny pulled the tab from the top of his root beer can, and the loud hiss reminded Libby of his presence. "Danny, you should move close here too. These rules apply to you as well as your dad, and there are several of them that I want to make sure you understand."

"Yes'm." Danny dragged his chair close and leaned over the desk. "I don't read so good yet, 'specially upside down."

Libby chuckled and turned the pages so both her guests could see them. "First of all, you need to understand the rule concerning guests. There is a ninety-day limit—"

"You'll be rid of us in sixty. Move on to the next one. What else?"

Libby felt her pulse quicken. "I wasn't thinking in terms of *getting rid* of you. It's simply a matter of—"

"The *rules!*" He finished her sentence for her. "This place has more rules than a convent!"

"Look, Mister. . .um. . .Greg, why don't you drop the armor and let's have a civil business discussion? If we can't be friends, at least I see no reason why we should be enemies. I think if we all try to understand—"

Libby never had a chance to finish her last sentence, because at that precise moment, a great swoosh of sticky brown liquid swept across her desk like a tidal wave, thoroughly dousing her papers with a dark ugly stain. An empty aluminum can rolled through the river of root beer and dropped with a clunk to the floor beside Libby's feet.

All three jumped up at once, and to Libby's credit, she did not scream. She very calmly pushed the button on her intercom. "Lorraine, could you please bring us a roll of paper towels? Quickly, please!" Rivulets of root beer streaked down her pale blue skirt, landing in big brown dots on her beige high-heeled pumps.

Greg stammered between apologies to Libby and reprimands to Danny. "Libby, I'm so sorry—Danny, how could you be so—here, let me see if we can salvage the papers." He held up the dripping documents and started another sticky stream.

Lorraine entered the room and gave a gasp. "What on earth. . .?" She began to pull off large sheets from the roll of paper towels, handed them to Libby and Greg, and all three of them went to work blotting the enlarging puddles of liquid calamity.

Greg's trousers, although not as drenched as Libby's skirt, were also splotched, causing him no small amount of embarrassment. Only Danny was as dry as a wad of cotton, as he backed his way toward the door.

"Oh, no you don't!" Greg shouted. "You get over here and help clean up this mess you created!"

Lorraine ran for a mop, and Libby momentarily forgot about her sodden skirt in a frantic effort to save the paperwork on her desk. At last, the room was restored to some semblance of order. Lorraine left the room carrying a waste can filled with soggy paper towels and a dripping mop, and Libby was left to handle the situation with Greg and Danny.

She fought to keep her cool, but it was difficult to retain her dignity with her skirt clinging tenaciously to her thighs. "Gentlemen," she began, "obviously this meeting cannot proceed today. We all need a change of clothes and time to calm down and make rational decisions. Perhaps we could try again tomorrow."

Greg's air of hostility seemed to vanish into thin air, replaced by a look that teetered between embarrassment and contrition. "Look, I'd like to make amends by starting over with a clean slate. I know it's asking a lot, Libby, but if you could bring a set of the rules by my condo, we could spread them out on the dining room table and go over them there where I can keep an eye on Danny in his own environment. I'll even make you a pot of coffee."

At this suggestion, the first thought that popped into Libby's mind was the warning Michael Phillips had issued before he left her office yesterday: *No fraternizing between staff and residents.* Of course, this would be strictly a matter of business, but she had to worry about how the situation might look to the other residents. She knew full well what a close eye they kept on everything that took place in the units around them. With Selena Watson's condo just across the courtyard from Greg's, she could scarcely hope that a visit, no matter how innocent, would go unnoticed.

Her position here at Blue Dolphin was already in jeopardy. She could not afford to risk fueling any damaging rumors. Being seen inside Greg's condo was the last thing Libby wanted, and yet what were her options? Danny was an accident just waiting to happen, and better to have it happen at his own house than in her office again. "All right, Greg, I'll have a set of the rules printed up to bring by your condo, but skip the coffee. I think I won't come in. I'll just highlight the points I think you and Danny should give extra consideration, and we can discuss them briefly at the door."

"Whatever you say. You're the boss." Greg gave her a maddening little salute before he took his son by the hand and led him toward the door.

Libby watched them walk away together, and wondered how such an innocent-looking pair could create such havoc! Her skirt was beginning to dry and stick to her legs like adhesive tape. She couldn't do anything until she changed into clean clothes. She was supposed to remain on the property until four o'clock, but today she would have to leave and go home a few minutes early. This would teach her to bring a spare set of clothes to keep in the office for emergency situations!

Pulling her purse from the desk drawer, she fished through

its contents for her car keys. "Lorraine," she said on her way through the outer office, "if any of the residents come looking for me, just tell them I had a small emergency and had to leave a few minutes early. I'm sorry to duck out on you this way, but I'll be back on the job bright and early tomorrow morning."

Lorraine gave her an understanding smile. "Don't worry about a thing, Libby. I'll hold things together here. And if you want the job of managing this place, I'll pray you get it, because you surely deserve it. But for the record, I wouldn't have your job for all the tea in China!"

three

Libby pulled her car into the narrow drive of the modest ranch house she shared with her sister, Celia. Pastel petunias bordered the sidewalk and bobbed gently in the late afternoon breeze, and freshly mown grass surrounded the house like an emerald sea. Libby was constantly amazed that, in a neighborhood where all the houses stood in rows like identical eggs in a carton, Celia somehow managed to make their home stand out among the rest.

Juggling night school and a full-time job as cashier at a local café, Celia was a never-complaining bundle of perpetual motion. How she ever found the time or energy to do yard work remained an eternal mystery to Libby. She admired Celia more than anyone else she had ever known, but she did worry about her. Celia had become so thin that her clothes fell loosely around her meager frame, and dark shadows lingered beneath her eyes.

Celia had protested when Libby suggested she have a checkup. "There's nothing wrong with me that sleep won't cure, and I'll catch up on that between semesters. You'll see."

But semesters had come and gone, and all Libby could see was further weight loss and deepening shadows around Celia's eyes. At last Libby had forced her position by calling Dr. Jennings and making the appointment for Celia's checkup herself. If it turned out her sister was in good health as she continued to insist, then at least Libby would be relieved of that worry.

Libby hurried up the walk, hoping her neighbors were too busy to be peeking out their windows in the late afternoon. She could only imagine how she must look in her stained, sticky clothing!

When Libby walked through the front door, she wasn't given time to explain her unorthodox appearance before Celia exclaimed, "What in the world happened to you?" With her hands on her hips, her eyes bulged as big and round as two blue marbles.

At twenty-seven, Celia was only three years older than Libby, but for as long as Libby could remember, Celia had always hovered over her like a mother hen. Orphaned at a young age by a drunk driver, the two little girls had formed a strong bond early on that only grew deeper as they matured into womanhood. Celia had sacrificed her own opportunity for an education to see that Libby completed hers. Now Libby felt it was payback time.

The raise in salary that would accompany Libby's promotion to manager of Blue Dolphin would make it possible for Celia to quit her job at the café. She could attend school full time and complete her accounting degree in months instead of years. Libby longed to give her sister that chance.

Eyeing the shocked expression on Celia's face, Libby giggled in spite of her despair. "I think I just grabbed hold of a sixty-pound stick of dynamite!"

"Oh, Honey, you just had that skirt cleaned! What really happened? Are you okay?"

"I'm fine. I'll tell you all about it later. After I've had a shower and a change of clothes, I'll tell you a story you won't believe!"

Libby headed toward the bathroom, determined not to let her doom-and-gloom spirits spill over onto the person she loved most in the world. She'd try to make a joke of everything that had happened, no matter what she was feeling on the inside.

As warm water splashed over her body, Libby allowed her anxiety to surface. What would she do if Michael Phillips brought in someone new as manager of Blue Dolphin? Would it mean she had failed? At best, it would mean she was knocking herself out every day in a dead-end job with no future in sight. Perhaps she should consider leaving Four Star and placing an application with another management firm. *Dear Lord,* she prayed, *I need Your direction. Please help me make the best decisions for everyone concerned.*

With renewed determination, Libby scrubbed away the last traces of root beer from her body and made up her mind to fight for a job that was rightfully hers. She was the logical choice for that job—a job she knew she could do perfectly well—and she would refuse to cave in to the pressures of a few dissidents who tried to stand in her way.

Of course, it went without saying that she would continue to perform her obligations to the best of her ability, just the way Jake Wilkowski would have expected her to do. But even beyond that, she would go the second mile by making a special effort to avoid anything that would even *appear* to be negligent or improper.

That episode with Greg Cunningham and his son was a good example of the kind of thing she must avoid at all costs. It certainly did not add to her professional image, and she'd have to take steps to prevent a recurrence.

She was glad arrangements were in place to discuss the bylaws with the two of them. Greg seemed like a reasonable person, and perhaps she could come up with some suggestion that would keep Danny safely occupied for the remainder of their tenancy in Blue Dolphin.

Feeling better already, she stepped from the shower and toweled her body dry before slipping into a pair of denim shorts and a hot pink T-shirt. She now felt ready to sit down with Celia and give her a slightly diluted version of the last two days.

There would be no need to burden her sister with what had happened at the property owners' meeting yesterday morning. Celia already assumed Libby would move up into the vacancy created by Jake's death, and Libby would not tell her otherwise until a decision had been made. She would simply give her sister an account of the frog incident, making it sound amusing rather than serious. Then she would tell her about the meeting with Danny and his dad, and about the spilled root beer that was responsible for her soiled skirt. But she would not tell her Greg Cunningham had the clearest, bluest eyes she had ever seen. Why had she even thought of such a thing at a time like this?

꼬

"Whatever got into you today, Danny? I thought you promised to be on your best behavior!" Greg followed his son into the condo and closed the door behind them.

"You know I didn't mean to spill my root beer, Dad. It was an accident. I'm just a kid, you know, and kids aren't perfect. Besides, I don't see why I should even have to go to all these stupid meetings in the first place."

"You went yesterday morning because I had no one to watch you, and Miss Libby asked to have you come with me to her office this afternoon because of all the trouble you caused in the clubhouse yesterday morning. See how one bad decision can have a domino effect?"

"What's domino-fect?"

"You know—how we line up the dominoes and push the first one, and then they all tumble down. That's what happens with bad choices."

"I said I'm sorry, Dad." Danny sniveled, rubbing his knuckles across his eyes. "What else do you want me to do?"

His words hit Greg's heart like a warm summer rain. He put an arm around Danny's narrow shoulders and gave him a gentle squeeze. "I know it was an accident, Son, and you're right. You shouldn't even be a part of all this crazy condominium mania." Before the meeting yesterday morning, Greg had tried to engage the services of Mrs. Murphy, the sweet little old lady who lived in the unit below them, but it happened to be the morning her bridge group met. She had even offered to cancel and find a substitute for her bridge game, but Greg knew that would have been an imposition at the last minute. He should have spoken to Mrs. Murphy earlier.

She was always so willing to sit with Danny, and Danny actually seemed to like her because she played games with him and gave him chocolate chip cookies. And Greg was sure the woman appreciated the small amount of money she earned to supplement her Social Security income. He held a fleeting thought that Mrs. Murphy would not have even flinched at the sight of a harmless little frog. "It's okay, Buddy. Say, you never did get to have that soda. Go see if there's one in the fridge, and bring one out for me too."

Danny shuffled off to the kitchen, and Greg sat down at the couch to wait for him to return with the drinks. His root beer-splotched pants, although now dry, were stiff and uncomfortable, but he needed to have a little father-son talk. He had another "surprise" to spring on his son, and he was sure Danny was not going to like this one.

He could hear Danny popping the tabs on the cans, and he tried to decide how best to broach the subject. "Come on in here and sit beside me. We'll have time to cool off with our drinks before we take showers and get ready to go out tonight."

Danny almost dropped his can of soda for the second time of the day. "Go out? I want to watch the baseball game on TV tonight. I thought you wanted to see it too."

"Well, yeah, I did, but Tiffany called and she wants us both to come over to her house for dinner. Says she's cooking up something special just for us—some new recipe she found in one of her magazines. Hey, we could use some good home cooking, couldn't we? Aren't you getting tired of your old man's macaroni and cheese delights?"

"We could just have hot dogs. They go good with baseball games." Danny's plea carried a hopeless tone, as though he knew he had lost the battle already.

"Good idea! We'll do that tomorrow night! But let's go over and find out for ourselves if Tiffany is really the good cook she claims to be."

"And supposin' she is? Does that mean you're gonna ask her to get married and come live with us in our new house?"

"Will you get off that marriage kick? You must have been watching those afternoon soap operas, the way you keep bringing that subject up." Greg gave his son a playful jab on the shoulder. "You know you're not supposed to watch those silly things."

Greg's attempts to change the subject did little to appease Danny, who stormed out of the room and put his soda can in the recycle bin, mumbling all the way. "I'm not hungry for whatever it is Tiffany is fixin'. I'd rather have a plain ole hot dog."

Greg stared at the ceiling as though seeking divine guidance from an invisible source. What was he to do? He was fortunate the engineering firm that employed him was willing to let him do most of his work from his house. That would be even easier once his new house was finished and he had a big airy studio instead of a cramped corner of his mother's condominium.

But what about his son? Danny was the dearest person in the world to him. He couldn't imagine a day-to-day existence without him. And yet, as the years rolled by, Greg became more and more aware of Danny's need for maternal love and guidance.

Greg's mother had offered many times to move in with them to help with Danny's care. In fact, it was for that very reason that Greg had made the decision to settle in Florida where he could be near enough to utilize his mother's experience and advice without imposing on her. But Greg knew how much she enjoyed her independence, and he wouldn't allow her to alter her lifestyle just for his convenience.

His mother would soon be returning to her winter home here in Blue Dolphin, and he and Danny would be moving into their new house on the other side of town. That would be the best arrangement for everyone concerned, he was sure, but it did not solve his biggest problem. It was becoming more and more apparent to him that Danny needed a woman in the house—not just a housekeeper, but a full-time mother. Surprisingly, even Danny himself had often complained recently that he missed having a mother figure like all of his friends. That's what made Danny's dislike of Tiffany so puzzling.

Greg had no doubt that when his mother returned, she would be up to her old matchmaking tricks, introducing him to the daughters of her friends, or the women at the bank, or her doctor's nurse. Her attempts to make these meetings appear accidental bordered on comical, but Greg could not resent them when he knew they were born of love.

Although he would never admit this to his mother or to anyone else, he did long for a home complete with a wife and children. What normal man would not? The few brief years he had spent with Dianne had been the happiest time of his life, especially when Danny came to round out their family circle.

Since Dianne's untimely death, he had not found any woman with whom he could imagine sharing the rest of his life. Would Tiffany turn out to be that special person for him and for Danny? Besides being gregarious and fun, she was quite pretty and intelligent. Only time would tell how this chapter of his life would play out.

Greg pushed himself up from the couch and plumped the pillows crumpled by the weight of his body. "Hurry up, Danny. Go get in the shower. Use plenty of soap, and don't leave your towel on the floor."

❧

"Now remember, Danny, I want you to be on your best behavior tonight—no funny stuff!" Greg instructed as they rode the elevator to Tiffany's fourth-floor apartment. "Tiffany told me she's making a special Italian recipe, and I think she's gone to a lot of trouble for us. I want her to know we appreciate it."

"I'd still rather have hot dogs!" Danny mumbled, as the elevator ground to a halt and the doors yawned open. But he trudged dutifully down the hall behind his father to the door marked 4-B.

Greg carried a spring bouquet in his right hand and used his left to take a swipe at the stubborn red cowlick on Danny's head before he rang the doorbell.

After a short wait, the door opened, revealing their hostess in a shimmering black satin cocktail dress, her closely contoured skirt split to just above the knee. "Come in and make yourselves comfortable," Tiffany crooned, tossing her head so that her platinum blond hair swirled softly around her slender shoulders. She accepted the proffered flowers, smiled, and lifted her lips to offer a kiss. After Greg gave her a quick peck, she turned her attention to Danny. She raised her voice two tones. "And my goodness, just look at this little gentleman. Doesn't he look smart?" She leaned down to plant a kiss on his cheek, but Danny dodged her lips by scooting to one side. He cast his eyes around the room.

"This place is swell, Tiffany. Can I turn on your TV?"

"Danny!" Greg's tone said a great deal more than his word, and Danny snapped to attention.

"I mean, just in case you wanted to get me out of your way or something, I could just sit here real quiet and watch that ole ball game that's on. Course, if you want me to help you do something, I'd be happy to, Ma'am."

Greg nodded his approval, and Tiffany was quick on the uptake. "I'll turn the television on for you after dinner, Danny, but first, come over here and sit beside me on the couch."

Tiffany led the way across the room, her high heels sinking soundlessly into the deep plush of the snow white carpet. "I thought we'd all have a little drink to get us started. What would you like, Danny? Would you like a can of cola?"

"Yes, Ma'am—" Danny's words were interrupted by a quick jab of his father's elbow. "No, Ma'am, I think I'd just like a drink of water."

"Me too," Greg echoed. "I'd just like water too, Tiff. It's

been really hot today, and a glass of ice water would be just right."

Tiffany gave them both a skeptical look, but hurried off to the kitchen. "I'll be right back," she promised.

While she was out of the room, Greg gave his son an encouraging smile. "You're doing great, Buddy. Now, when we get to the table, be very careful not to spill anything. And try to think of nice things to say about the dinner. Okay?"

"Sure, Dad. I can do that. But remember, tomorrow night we get to have hot dogs. You promised!"

"You got 'em!"

Tiffany returned from the kitchen with three glasses of water balanced on a silver tray, and to Greg's great relief, Danny managed to drink his entire glass of water without spilling a single drop. Tiffany excused herself to put the finishing touches on dinner, and at last the three of them were seated around her dining table.

Greg eyed the delicate lace tablecloth and fine crystal goblets and hoped Danny could make it through the meal without a catastrophe.

The first course was a shrimp cocktail. Seeing that Danny was watching his every move, trying to do things just right, Greg lifted his small fork and proceeded to enjoy one of his favorite foods. "Mmm, delicious!"

Tiffany beamed. "I'm glad you like it, Greg." Her long red lacquered nails glistened in the candlelight. "And how about you, Danny?"

Danny, taking his cue, selected his small fork, speared a shrimp and lifted it halfway to his mouth. He held the pink morsel aloft and gave it a look of approval. "Yes'm, this looks mighty nice. Kinda reminds me of last Saturday when my dad took me fishing."

Greg cringed. What in the world was in Danny's mind? But he did not have to wonder long, because Danny continued holding his shrimp in the air and explained. "We got us a whole bucket of these little fellers, and squished that hook right down the middle of 'em. Man, the fish just—"

"Danny! That's enough!"

"I was just—"

"Enough! Eat your shrimp." Greg shot an apologetic smile in Tiffany's direction and noted that she had removed her fork from her bowl and placed it on the side of her plate.

"I think I'd better check on the casserole," she said, rising from her seat and hurrying to the kitchen.

Danny finished his last shrimp and wiped his lips on his linen napkin as Tiffany returned to the dining room. "That sure was good, Tiffany!"

"Well, I'm glad you enjoyed it, Danny." When Tiffany carried the iced bowls to the kitchen, Greg noted that hers was still almost full of untouched shrimp.

Taking advantage of her brief absence, Greg whispered to Danny, "I thought I told you to say something *nice* about the meal."

"Well, I did. That was the nicest thing I could think of, 'cause goin' fishing is just about the nicest thing in the whole world. I meant it as a compliment, Dad!"

"Okay, well, you'll have another chance to try again in a minute. Shh! Here she comes."

Tiffany placed a steaming casserole—angel hair spaghetti bathed in a rich Alfredo sauce—in the center of the dining table, resting it on a gleaming silver trivet. She added a bowl of tossed salad and a loaf of warm Italian bread.

"Just look at that!" Greg exclaimed, rubbing his hands together. "You're really going to spoil us with food like this, Tiffany!" Taking no chances, he ladled a portion onto Danny's dinner plate before helping himself to a generous serving of the casserole.

Greg noted that Tiffany had become very quiet. Trying to stimulate conversation, he complimented her on the excellence of the dinner. "Danny and I don't get such elegant meals at home, do we, Son?"

"No, Sir." Danny too was subdued, his eyes lowered to his plate.

At last Tiffany broke the silence. "Danny, tell me what you like to do when you're not in school. Do you belong to the Boy Scouts?"

"No, Ma'am. Not yet. I'm not old enough. Mostly I just like to do stuff with my dad." In an obvious effort to right whatever wrong he had committed earlier, he offered, "I'm sorry I talked about the shrimp. I didn't know I wasn't supposed to, but I really liked it a lot."

"That's all right, Danny. I'm glad you enjoyed it. And fishing sounds like fun. Maybe you will let me come along with you some time."

"Yes'm, maybe you might like it. We wouldn't even have to use shrimp."

Danny held up a strand of the spaghetti with his fork and eyed it pensively as it swayed back and forth in midair. "Sometimes we just dig us up some wor—"

Greg anticipated what was coming but could not stop it in time. *"Danny!"*

But Danny didn't miss a beat. Letting his spaghetti slide back onto his plate, he tried again. "We wouldn't even have to fish. Sometimes we just go for a boat ride. I reckon you'd probably like that better."

Greg glanced sidewise at Tiffany and noted the green pallor of her cheeks. Turning his attention back to his son, he instructed Danny to finish the rest of his meal in silence. "Not another word until you're through."

There was little conversation during the remainder of the meal. When at last they were through, Greg made an effort to mend his fences. "I'll clear the table and help you clean up."

"You don't have to do that," she demurred.

"I can help too!" Danny offered, balancing a fragile crystal goblet on his salad plate as he rose from his seat.

"No!" Tiffany exclaimed, reaching for the teetering glass. "I mean, I wouldn't hear of having my guests help. And Greg, I hate to admit it, but I do have a headache, and I have to get up early in the morning. I hope you won't be disappointed if we call it a night."

"Not at all," Greg said. He could certainly recognize a classic brush-off, and his pride would not have allowed him to protest, even if he had wanted to. "As a matter of fact, Danny and I have a couple of things we need to take care of tonight, so if you'll excuse us. . ."

"Call me tomorrow?" Tiffany purred.

Greg moved toward the door, pulling Danny by the arm. "Thank you for a delicious meal, Tiff. Danny, don't you have something to say?"

"Oh, yeah. It was real good, Tiffany. Thanks a lot for inviting us." His words tumbled out fast as his eyes focused on the living room wall clock, and Greg knew he was checking out the time for that ball game.

Tiffany followed them to the foyer and stood with her face upturned, but Greg pushed his son through the door and followed him into the hall. "Good night, Tiffany. Thanks for everything."

four

Almost thirty minutes ahead of schedule, Libby Malone was the first of the staff to arrive at the Blue Dolphin administration building. Having left work fifteen minutes early the afternoon before, she was determined to get a head start on the day.

Libby angled her car into the space reserved for the property manager—Jake's space. She still thought of it as that; she just couldn't help herself. Jake Wilkowski would always be an important part of her life.

The most wonderful gift Jake had given to her had nothing at all to do with property management. Before she met him, she would have assured anyone who asked that she was a Christian. Of course she was! She and Celia had gone to Sunday school regularly as children. Even during her college years, she had attended Sunday services whenever she could; but between studies and social obligations, there just wasn't much time for "extra activities."

Libby's priorities were of great concern to Celia during this period, and all of Celia's letters were filled with spiritual encouragement for her younger sister. But Libby's answer was always the same: "I just don't have time to think about things like that right now, Celia. I'm working so hard to keep up with my classes. Please don't pressure me about anything else right now." And after she graduated, it was the pressures of work that occupied her mind and filled her days.

When Jake and his wife had first invited Libby to their church on Sunday and for dinner afterward, she had felt obligated to accept their invitation. After all, Jake was her immediate supervisor, and she wanted desperately to make a good impression on him. Little did she realize that day, as she walked between Jake and Elvira Wilkowski into the beautiful sanctuary and sat beside them in the pew, that her life would be forever changed.

As she listened to the words of the minister and joined in singing the traditional hymns, something happened to her that she could only partially understand. A strange warmth swept through her body, and as though a veil were being lifted from her heart, she felt God's presence in a new and personal way, and she had responded to His call.

At the close of the service, her knees felt like wet cardboard as she walked down the aisle to kneel at the altar. Against a background of organ chimes, she poured out her heart to the Lord, and He wrapped her in His loving arms while she wept. Later, when she lifted her head, she realized Jake and Elvira were kneeling on either side of her, their smiling faces streaked with tears.

No one could have been more pleased about this conversion than Celia. At last Libby had learned to open her heart to the Lord, and the bond shared between the two sisters, rooted in Christ's love, now became more firmly cemented than ever.

In the days and months that followed, Libby came to realize that Jake was much more than a "Sunday Christian." He lived his faith without compromise every minute of his life. To Libby, he became a father figure as well as a friend and a boss, and he was never too busy to give her bits of his sage advice. Wasn't it ironic, then, that he had plunged her into the biggest controversy she had ever encountered?

She locked her car and crossed the grass on concrete stepping-stones, using her key to open the front office door. *Bless Lorraine!* She had wiped away every trace of yesterday's accident and had even sprayed the room with a fragrance that masked any lingering scent of root beer. No one coming into the office would ever guess the catastrophic events of yesterday.

As upsetting as the experience had been at the time, in

retrospect Libby could not resist a chuckle. Danny was a handful, no doubt about that, but something about the little boy seemed to tug at her heartstrings.

It wasn't Danny's fault that his temporary home was in the midst of aging adults, in a place where every amenity was geared to geriatric pleasures and safety. How bored the child must be with no friends and playmates his own age. The new school year would begin next week, and perhaps Danny would develop some new friends and interests.

Libby entered her private office, leaving the door ajar so she could keep an eye on the outer office until Lorraine arrived. She pulled her "to do" list from her top desk drawer and began to plan her day. At the top of the page were two jobs she could delegate to her secretary: *Get bids for the sidewalk repair in front of building 410,* and *Order sealer and paint for the maintenance shop.* Further down the page, she frowned at one of the items: *Meet with Greg Cunningham and Danny.* She would ask Lorraine to call for an appointment to get that little chore out of the way as early as possible.

She heard the front door open, followed by her secretary's cheery "Hello!"

"Hello yourself. You sure did a bang-up job on this office before you left yesterday. Thanks, Lorraine. I don't know what any of us would do around here without you."

Lorraine clicked across the hardwood floor and deposited her purse in her bottom desk drawer. "Glad I could help." She moved toward Libby's open doorway. "But don't give me too much credit. I don't think I did a very professional job of maintaining the peace around here after you left yesterday."

Libby's eyes widened in apprehension. "What happened?"

"Oh, that Watson lady came storming in here just five minutes after you left, demanding to see you. When I told her you had gone home for the day, she hit the ceiling. I tried to explain your emergency, but she refused to listen to reason. She just kept going on about dependability and maturity and all that. She left without giving me a chance to tell her what really happened, and the last thing she said as she sashayed out the front door was that she intended to call Michael Phillips immediately to inform him of your absence. Just thought I'd better warn you."

Libby's heart sank. Just one more nail in her coffin. What could happen next to jeopardize her position here at Blue Dolphin? "Thanks for the warning, Lorraine. I guess you'd better bring your notebook in here so we can go over today's work before the fireworks start."

≈

The "fireworks" started just thirty minutes later. Sitting across from Libby at her desk, Michael Phillips rubbed the furrows in his brow. "That woman was absolutely livid, Libby. I know it's not a crime for you to leave a few minutes early now and then. You certainly never complain about the many days you stay long after hours to clear up a problem, but I'm surprised you would take such a chance right now when things here are so tenuous. We'd just talked about the importance of dotting all your i's and crossing all your t's, at least until things settle down a bit."

Libby was annoyed that Michael did not give her the benefit of the doubt. She felt her past performance warranted that. She could easily explain the situation that had caused her to leave early, but since most of her problems had originated with Greg Cunningham and his son, she was hesitant to bring their names into the discussion again today. Instead she simply said, "I'm sorry, Michael. It was bad judgment on my part to leave before four yesterday, even though I did have a minor emergency. I'll try to do better in the future."

"Have you resolved the situation with the Cunninghams? I still don't quite understand how they've been allowed to move into a community restricted to senior citizens."

"They're temporary, Michael. The unit belongs to Greg's mother, and I thought I explained that he's using it while he's building a new house. His house won't be ready until November, but that will get him out of here under the ninety-day limit."

Michael shifted his position in his chair and leaned forward on his elbows. "And what if there's a construction delay? Does he understand the ninety-day limit on visitors?"

Libby pushed her pencil around in circles, scribbling meaningless doodles on a piece of scrap paper. "I met with them—I'm meeting with them today—to go over the Blue Dolphin bylaws and make sure they understand everything."

"I don't understand why this wasn't done in the beginning. Don't you interview all new residents before they move in?"

"Yes, of course. But remember, Greg and Danny aren't really residents." Why was Michael having such a hard time understanding that? "Technically, they're Mrs. Cunningham's guests. It is the owner's responsibility to inform guests of the rules and to see that they abide by them."

"Then perhaps you should call Mrs. Cunningham and discuss these problems with her. You do have her northern number, don't you?"

"Yes, I do, Michael. And if my meeting today with Greg and Danny doesn't set things straight, then I'll give her a call."

"Okay, Libby. I'm sure I don't need to remind you again how precarious your position here has become. You'll be under severe scrutiny until the management issue is resolved. I'll run over now and see Selena Watson, to try to placate her before our meeting with the board next week. Most of the board members are pretty reasonable people, but Selena's opinions seem to carry a lot of weight. It would be to your advantage not to antagonize her further."

Michael slid his chair back from the desk and stood looking down at the top of her bent head. "Libby, you and I both know you're capable of handling this job, but are you sure you really want it?"

Libby did not hesitate for an instant. "Yes, Michael, I'm

very sure. I–I can't begin to tell you how much I want this promotion." Libby struggled to control her voice. Thinking of Celia and the things she hoped to do for her, she added, "And besides, Michael, I–I really *need* it."

"Then I'll do everything I can to help you."

Libby watched him leave her office and knew he meant what he said. He would do everything he could to help her, but would it be enough?

❧

Libby rang the doorbell of the Cunningham condo and wondered if she only imagined a movement of the window drapes in the condo across the courtyard. She had arranged this meeting with Greg and Danny to go over the Blue Dolphin bylaws in hopes of putting to rest some of the unease surrounding their occupancy. She gripped the handles of her briefcase with a nervous urgency when she heard footsteps approaching the door.

"Come in, come in. Danny and I have been looking for you."

Libby shifted her briefcase to her left hand in order to respond to Greg's outstretched hand. His grip was firm and warm, a warmth that seemed to radiate up her arm all the way to her shoulders. Annoyed at her own reaction, she pulled her hand from his and forced her attention to the job at hand instead of on Greg's sparkling blue eyes.

Greg held the door wide, inviting Libby to step into the foyer, but remembering her earlier resolve, she shook her head. "No, this shouldn't take long. Let's just take a look at these bylaws right out here on the balcony. Libby balanced her briefcase on the porch rail and unsnapped its latch. As soon as she raised the lid, a sudden flurry of summer air caught up the top paper and sent it spiraling skyward. "Oh no!" She slammed the case shut, while Greg went scurrying down the steps to retrieve the flying paper.

In minutes, he returned, taking the steps two at a time, and handed the elusive document to Libby. "It's foolish trying to work out here on the porch when I have a perfectly good table right here in the dining room. Come on inside."

Libby surveyed her surroundings for a better solution, but seeing none, she reluctantly agreed.

Libby looked around the mirrored living room. *Surprisingly neat for a bachelor and his son,* she thought. "I have only a few minutes, Greg, so if we could get right down to business. . ."

"Of course." Greg pulled out one of the dining room chairs. "Sit right here at the table. I've just made a pot of fresh coffee. . ." He disappeared into the kitchen before Libby could voice her protest. Did he think she had come here for a social call?

She opened her briefcase and spread her papers on the table in front of her, assuming her most professional manner.

Greg returned to the room and set a porcelain cup and saucer in front of her. "Cream and sugar?"

"No thanks. Just black. This shouldn't take long," she declared again, making a few notes with her pen. "Is Danny here? I want him to be a part of this."

"Danny," he called. "Come in here, Son, on the double. There's a lady here who'd like to see you."

Danny came down the hall at a speed that could hardly be classified as "on the double," but he greeted Libby with a fleeting smile and took one of the chairs across from his dad. He positioned his elbows on the table and propped his chin in his hands, fixing his eyes on Libby with such an intensity that she found it disarming.

"Now, Danny, there's nothing to be nervous about," Libby assured him, trying to interpret his unrelenting stare.

"Oh, I'm not nervous, Ma'am. I'm just listenin'. But you gotta be careful around here, cause we been havin' a terrible lot of trouble with big black poison spiders."

Libby's eyebrows shot up into a questioning arch.

"Danny, what's gotten into you?" Greg asked. "You know we don't—"

"Look out!" Danny shrieked, pointing to the rug beneath Libby's feet.

Libby fell right into the trap, twisting around to see the floor. Although her first impulse was to scream, it only took her an instant to recognize the black rubber spider for what it was—a harmless toy meant to scare her out of her wits. She could only laugh. She leaned over, picked up the ugly creature, and held it aloft. "Pretty realistic looking, Danny. I might have actually been fooled if I hadn't owned one of these things myself when I was about your age. Seven, isn't it?"

Greg had risen from his seat, his face scarlet with embarrassment. "Danny, take that thing out of here this minute. Didn't I tell you not to try any of your tricks today? We'll talk about this later, Son. Now, go put that thing in your room and come back here and try to behave like a gentleman."

While Danny was out of the room, Greg tried to apologize. "I'm sorry, Libby. I declare, he's not a bad kid. This whole condominium thing has brought out some strange quirks in his personality."

"He's just a normal little boy, Greg. In fact, I find him extremely mature in some ways. He seems to have a vocabulary way beyond his years."

"I suppose that's because he's been in the company of adults for most of his life. Sometimes even *I* forget he's just a little boy."

"Well, I hope you won't punish him for that bit of mischief. I tried the same thing myself when I was a little girl. Actually, it's kind of flattering."

"Flattering? How do you figure that?"

"Well, you don't joke around with people you dislike. I think Danny was just testing me a bit, and showing me we can be friends if I pass the test."

Greg sat down again and took a swallow of his hot coffee. "Okay. I see what you mean. And you sure passed the test. Thanks for not fainting or anything. Here comes Danny again, and I'll wager he'll be properly subdued this time."

Danny, with an angelic look on his face took his place at the table. "Sorry, Miss Libby. It was just a joke."

"I know, Danny. I enjoy jokes. But now, let's get down to some serious business."

One by one, Libby read the condominium bylaws and discussed their importance. She could tell by Greg's bored expression that he felt she was talking down to him, as though he were a kindergarten student and she the overbearing teacher. Surprisingly, however, Danny sat at rapt attention, his eyes fastened on Libby's face as though he wanted to memorize her features for future recall. She could almost see the wheels whizzing around in his seven-year-old brain, and wished she could discern just what kind of plan he was preparing to spring on her next. She was certain he had more on his mind than condo rules.

"Danny, do you have any questions?" she asked, hoping to gain some insight into his thoughts.

Danny took a few moments to ponder his answer, but at last he said, "Yes'm, actually, I do."

"Well, go ahead. Ask anything you want, and I'll do my best to answer."

"I was just wonderin' if—do you like baseball?"

Libby saw the stern warning look Greg aimed at his son, but she had no idea what Danny's question meant, nor why it should have displeased his father. "Why, yes, as a matter of fact, I do like baseball. But is that what you really wanted to ask me?"

"Well. . .what about fishin'?" Danny asked after a thoughtful pause. "Can you bait your own hook?"

Greg stood up abruptly, almost spilling his coffee. "Danny, if Libby is finished with us, you need to go clean up your room."

"But, Dad, I already—"

"Now!"

Libby gathered her papers into her briefcase. "I think we're through here, and I really do need to get back to the office. I hope we all understand each other better now." But in truth, Libby did not understand at all. What was Danny talking about? Baseball? Fishing? And why did Greg so obviously quiet him and send him to his room? No, she did not understand this strange male twosome at all.

Greg walked her to the door. "Yes, I think this time has been very enlightening, and Danny and I will both try to be on our best behavior. But if we slip up anywhere, I'm sure you'll be quick to let us know."

Was there a touch of sarcasm in his statement, or was he sincere? Libby wondered how Greg could feel so "enlightened," when she felt so totally confused.

five

"Well, how did the meeting go?" Lorraine asked when Libby returned to the administration office. "Did you and that handsome hunk of a man have a confrontation?"

"Not at all," Libby assured her, laughing. "It was all quite civilized. I think we understand each other better now. Were there any calls for me while I was out?"

"You don't want to know."

"Uh-oh. What now?" Libby stopped in front of Lorraine's desk and wondered what her next challenge would be. Had the irrigation system malfunctioned again?

"First Mr. Blake in building 210 called to report the lawn maintenance service had not properly pruned the hibiscus bushes by his unit. He says they are still too tall and are blocking his view of the lake."

Libby heaved a sigh of relief. "Is that all? That's easy to take care of. I'll simply have lawn maintenance go back on Monday and trim them a little more."

"No, that's *not* all. Five minutes later, Mavis Benchley called from the condo next door to him, to complain the lawn maintenance people just butchered the beautiful hibiscus bushes. She says she's been crying all afternoon because they cut off all the pretty blossoms." Smiling, Lorraine handed the two complaint slips to Libby. "Here. Go in your office, close the door, and scream real loud. I promise I won't tell a soul."

Libby laughed. Lorraine always knew how to help her see the lighter side of things. Later in the day, she would drive the condo golf cart over to building 210 and try to talk to both of the dissidents. Each of the twenty buildings in Blue

Dolphin contained twenty condos, and sometimes it was difficult to get all the residents to see things the same way, but maybe they could all come to some kind of agreement.

She took her briefcase into her private office and returned the printout of condominium bylaws to the filing cabinet. She had dreaded that meeting with Greg and his son today, but actually it had been quite pleasant.

There was something magnetic about Greg Cunningham. Lorraine had referred to him as a "handsome hunk." But it was more than just his physical appearance. Libby liked the way he looked her right in the eye when he talked to her, as though she were the only person in the world who had his attention.

During her brief visit, she had been pleased to note that the Bible on his desk bore his name in gold, and not a speck of dust on the cover to suggest its dormancy. *He must be a Christian,* she decided. At the right place and at the right time, she might even be attracted to him. But of course, this was *not* the right time, and it certainly wasn't the right place, with Four Star's strict policy against fraternization between staff and residents looming over her. That seemed like a rather silly rule to Libby, but nevertheless, as interim manager, it was her job not only to enforce the rules set by the board, but to abide by them as well.

Anyway, she had enough to think about these days just trying to keep things running smoothly at Blue Dolphin. At the moment, there was no time in her life for romance, and that was a fact she'd better not forget.

She pushed all thoughts of Greg Cunningham out of her mind and pulled her expense ledger out of the file.

❧

"Just what was that little pop quiz all about?" Greg asked his son as soon as Libby was out of hearing distance. "What is it you're trying to orchestrate, Danny?"

"Aw, Dad, you know I don't know nothin' about music.

What are you talkin' about?"

"Come on, Danny. Don't go into the 'innocent child routine' with me. Why were you giving Libby the third degree?"

"Dad, I gotta go finish cleanin' up my room. That's what you told me to do, remember?"

"Right. And because you're such a conscientious little boy, you can't wait to do as you were told." Greg drawled out his sarcasm in slow, carefully enunciated words, working hard to control the smile that lurked just beneath the surface of his lips. "But first we're going to talk about this other matter. I saw you looking at Libby, and I know what you had in mind, Danny, but it's not going to work. I appreciate your efforts to help, Son, but there are some things I have to work out by myself. You have to remember that *I'm* the parent here." He winked and smiled at his son to lighten the moment.

"Dad, all I did was try to help us get to know Miss Libby a little better. You told me to be nice and polite to her. I just wanted to find out what kind of stuff she likes to do. What's wrong with that?"

"No harm in that," Greg admitted. He tilted his son's chin upward, forcing direct eye contact. "But listen carefully, Danny. I choose my own friends, and I don't need any matchmaking help. I'll get plenty of that soon enough when your grandma gets here. Now, don't you start in on me too. Okay, Buddy?"

"Okay, Dad. But you gotta admit Libby's a whole lot more fun than Tiffany." Danny's giggle bubbled up in spite of his father's serious expression. "Ole Tiffany woulda flat-out died over that spider."

"Danny, you know you're not allowed to speak disrespectfully of grown-ups." Greg tried to swallow the grin that spread across his lips, but he couldn't do it. Danny just cracked him up sometimes. And the picture of Tiffany with a spider at her feet didn't do a thing to help him conceal his amusement. "Okay, Danny. You've made your point, but just remember what I said. Now, go finish cleaning your room."

ò&

Libby set one of her bags of groceries on the porch, freeing her right hand to open the front door. "Hi, Celia! I'm home," she called, reaching back to retrieve her package. With her purse slung over one shoulder and both arms filled with groceries, she headed straight for the kitchen.

Celia stood at the kitchen window staring out into the yard, and Libby knew at once that something was wrong. She placed her bags on the countertop. "What is it, Celia?" Her heart plummeted with the sudden recollection that this was the day Celia was scheduled to visit the clinic for her checkup. "What did Dr. Jennings say?"

Celia pasted an obviously fake smile on her face. "Well, those doctors just don't know everything, do they? If I had anything seriously wrong with me, I wouldn't feel this good now, would I?"

"Tell me, Celia. What did he say?" Libby persisted in a voice that forbade evasion.

Celia's face contorted, and her pretenses fell like sudden summer rain. "He found a lump in my breast, Libby. He says it looks suspicious, and he wants me to have surgery as soon as possible. I tried to explain that I just can't do that right now, what with my work and school and all, but I promised to think about it and call him."

Celia's expression told Libby her sister was much more concerned than she wanted to admit. She wasn't at all sure Celia had told her the whole story.

"Call him tomorrow, Celia. Tell him to set up the operation as soon as possible. This has to be our first priority. You can worry about making up the schoolwork later. And as for the job, Mr. McKenzie will surely understand. You can't afford to put this off a single day." Libby gathered her sister in her arms. "Don't you know how important you are to me? We'll do whatever the doctors advise, and beyond that, we'll put ourselves in God's hands and pray."

Celia squeezed Libby and let her tears fall. "I knew I'd feel better about everything as soon as you got home and let me unburden on your shoulders." She released her hold and dabbed at her eyes with a tissue pulled from her apron pocket. "Here, let's put these groceries away."

While the two women worked together in the kitchen, Libby prodded Celia for more details about the report from the doctor and his plans for the upcoming surgery.

"If the biopsy shows the tumor to be benign, then the operation will be relatively minor," Celia told her. "That's what I'm praying for."

"And it will be," Libby tried to reassure her. "Like you said earlier, you're much too energetic to have a serious illness."

"I'm just so thankful about your promotion," Celia said. "The expense of the surgery, coupled with my layoff from work, is going to put a terrible strain on our budget. At least with your new position, you'll be bringing in a hefty salary increase. I'm sorry I won't be carrying my weight for a while, but, Honey, I'll make this up to you some day. As soon as I get my accounting degree, I'll be able to have a *real* job, like you do."

Libby would never forget the long hours Celia had worked, putting all her own hopes and dreams on hold so Libby could get an education. "I don't want to hear that kind of talk. You *do* have a real job already, Celia. Your job right now is to take care of yourself, and that's all that matters."

Libby watched Celia stretch to put a box of cornflakes on the top shelf and thought for the thousandth time how thin and frail she looked.

Libby simply *had* to get that promotion! She had told Michael she needed the salary increase, but she had not realized at the time just how much would depend on it. Why was Selena Watson so arbitrary? It didn't seem fair that one person could get the whole condominium community stirred up over nothing.

But she couldn't burden Celia with her own concerns. Celia had enough to worry about already. Instead she said, "Go powder your nose, and let's go out on the town tonight. We'll grab a couple of burgers at that new fast-food place that opened around the corner last week. We'll forget all about doctors and work, and just have a girls' night out."

Celia's giggle was music to Libby's ears. *Dear Lord,* she prayed silently, *please help me take care of my sister. Enable me to provide for her the way she has always done for me for as long as I can remember.* "Hurry up so we can beat the evening crowds. I'll get my keys."

The two sisters walked hand in hand down the porch steps, each wearing a smile meant to hide her lines of worry and concern from the other.

six

When the next few days passed without incident, Libby began to breathe a bit easier. Now that school had started, she had seen Danny catching the bus by the front gate every morning, which meant he was gone all day until late afternoon.

Selena had not been seen or heard from in the administration office since last week, and contact with Michael Phillips had been limited to a daily phone call.

Celia's surgery was set for a week from Wednesday. But once that was behind them, barring any unfavorable medical report, Libby hoped her life might begin to return to a normal pattern.

Late Friday afternoon, she was tidying her desk to leave for the weekend when the buzzer on her intercom sounded.

"Yes, Lorraine?"

"It's Mr. Kalinski on line one. He lives over in building 300. He seems quite upset about something, and he insists on talking to you. I know you're trying to get away, but I think you'd better hear what he has to say."

"Thanks, Lorraine. I'll take it." Before she pressed the button connecting her to the blinking line, Libby ran her fingers through her hair in frustration. Why was it that most of her troubles seemed to come from building 300? That was where Selena lived, and Greg and Danny too. Whatever Mr. Kalinski's complaint, she hoped it was not related to the Cunninghams. She couldn't afford any more trouble from that corner!

"Hello, Mr. Kalinski," she answered in her brightest voice. "What can I do for you today, Sir?"

"It's not what you can do for *me;* it's what you'd *better* do about that kid before he puts somebody's eye out."

"Kid? Do you mean Danny? Is he causing trouble, Mr. Kalinski?"

"He's out in the backyard practicing casting with a rod and reel, and if that hook hits one of our residents, there's gonna be trouble aplenty. He shouldn't be out there without supervision in the first place; and in the second place, a fishhook is not a toy."

"I couldn't agree with you more, Mr. Kalinski. I'll see to it right away, and I appreciate your calling this to my attention."

"Humph!" The receiver slammed down on the other end and the line went dead.

Libby heaved a heavy sigh and grabbed the key to the electric golf cart. Running through the front office, she called over her shoulder to Lorraine, "I'll be back as soon as I can. If you leave before I get back, just put any messages for me on my desk. I'll check before I go home."

She did not linger long enough to hear Lorraine's reply. Like a teenager late for a date, she was out the front door and rolling down the drive in the Blue Dolphin golf cart.

She wheeled into the parking lot of building 300, jumped out and ran through the courtyard of the U-shaped edifice toward the backyard. Sure enough, just as Mr. Kalinski had reported, Danny stood with his right arm pulled back, and let the line fly off a shiny aluminum reel, sending a bright red fishing lure hurling through space. Libby watched it land in a patch of palmettos, and Danny scowled when he couldn't pull it loose.

"Hello, Danny," Libby called.

When he looked up and recognized her, Danny's scowl immediately turned into a wide, winsome grin. "Hiya, Miss Libby. Lemme get this line untangled and I'll show you how good I'm gettin' at this. I'm just about to get the hang of it."

Libby followed him to the palmetto clump and watched him work his line free. She was relieved to see that the red plastic lure he retrieved was only a small plastic fish with no hooks attached. "Looks like you're practicing for a big fishing trip," she said.

"Yep. Me and my dad are goin' out in the boat tomorrow. Dad says if I can catch one, we'll clean it and have it for supper. Do you like fish?"

"Sure do. Where is your dad now, Danny?"

Danny reeled in his line in preparation for his next cast. "He's inside workin'. I have to be real good so he can finish his work if I want him to take me fishin' tomorrow, so I'm stayin' out of his way."

The corners of Libby's mouth turned upward. Danny was such an appealing child! "I don't want to spoil your chances for a fishing trip, but do you suppose I might have a few moments with him?"

"Sure. I guess so. Just go up and knock on the door." Danny's disappointment registered in his eyes. Libby had not forgotten his request to watch his next cast.

"Tell you what, Danny. I'll wait long enough to watch you cast once more, and then maybe you'll go upstairs with me."

"Oh, boy! Yes'm. Now watch this. Here goes!" With that, the red lure sailed through the air again, this time landing on the grass where Danny had no trouble reeling it in. "How was that?"

"Just like a pro, Danny. I'm betting you catch at least one fish tomorrow. Now, let's go upstairs and see your dad."

Danny bounced up the concrete stairs with Libby close on his heels, but she declined his invitation to "come on in."

"Go tell your dad I'm here. I'd better wait outside until you get him."

While she waited, Libby smoothed her skirt and ran her fingers through her windblown hair, trying to coax it into some kind of order. At the end of the day, she was sure she must look a fright.

Greg came to the door in his stocking feet, a loose T-shirt pulled over his rolled-up blue jeans. His wary expression told her he feared the worst. "What now?" he asked without a trace of hospitality.

"I. . .um, just need a few minutes to talk to you, please. May I come in?" Although she didn't like the idea of going into his condo again, she didn't want to stand at the door in full view of the neighbors, some of whom she was sure were watching through cracks in their closed curtains.

Greg held the door open and Libby stepped inside. Without offering her a chair, he crossed his arms and said, "What brings you here this time, Miss Malone?"

"Please, Greg, don't go ballistic on me. Let's talk like two civilized adults. I've had a complaint about Danny and I'm—"

"That does it! Tomorrow I'm looking for another place to live," Greg exploded, his face red with rage. "What is it with these people?"

Danny stood close behind Greg's back, one hand clutching a leg of his father's denim britches while he peered around his backside.

"I was about to say that I'm not at all sure the complaint was justified, Greg. But I really can't talk to you when you're in such an obviously hostile mood."

Greg raked his hands through his dark hair and took a deep breath. "Okay, I'm sorry. Come sit down and tell me the latest problem."

Libby perched on the edge of the living room sofa and wondered how best to begin. "Well, it seems that some of your neighbors feel Danny should have adult supervision when he plays outside." She didn't mention about the casting. She could explain to Mr. Kalinski later that there were no hooks involved, and that the lure was very lightweight plastic. In an attempt to appease Greg's anger, she added, "They. . .um, don't want him to get hurt."

"Look here, Miss—"

"Libby, *please.*"

"Okay, then. Look here, *Libby.* I don't know how much

you know about growing boys, but believe me, seven-year-old boys do not need to have an adult hanging over their shoulders at every minute of the day. Now, Danny is a pretty dependable kid, and unless and until he proves otherwise, I am not going to punish him by curtailing his freedom. Is that clear?"

"It makes sense to me, Greg. I'm only the middle person in this scenario. But I'll have a talk with the resident in your building who turned in the complaint, and I'll try to explain your position. Fair enough?"

Greg's color was slowly returning to normal, but still he did not smile. "How do you stand it?" he asked.

"What do you mean?" Libby was genuinely puzzled by his question. "How do I stand what?"

"This place. All these stupid rules. And all these old people."

"Whoa, Greg. Not so fast. One question at a time. First of all, this place is as beautiful as any I've ever seen. Gorgeous landscaping, wild birds that eat out of your hand, lakes, and a river. . ."

"That's not what I mean."

"And the rules you think are stupid are all made to serve a purpose. When this many people live close together in a small area, they have to learn to adjust and compromise, Greg. To give and take."

"Forget I mentioned—"

"But the worst part of your comment had to do with your stereotyping of 'old people.' Do you really think age has anything to do with it? Why, some of the nicest people I know, including your own mother, are elderly, and some of the rudest and most selfish are people in our age bracket. It's like that verse in the Bible where it says something about there being diversities of gifts, but the same spirit. It goes on to tell how the body needs ears, and eyes, and feet, all to complement each other in serving the same purpose."

"I think that's in First Corinthians," Greg said thoughtfully.

"Okay, Libby. You make a good point." He looked slightly chagrined, but he held his ground. "Okay, so maybe I was being a little unfair. It's just that Danny and I are trying to do everything exactly the way we're supposed to, and it's like a thousand eyes are out there watching us, hoping we'll slip and make one little mistake."

Libby's lips curled upward in spite of her determination to remain in control of the situation. "No, not a thousand, Greg. But maybe a couple now and then," she admitted, glancing over her shoulder toward the window. "And believe me, I know that feeling all too well. I've been under the microscope myself these last few weeks."

Greg's look mellowed. "Right. I remember what a hard time some of them were giving you at that meeting the other day. I'm sorry if Danny and I have added to your problems, but we'll be out of here soon, and you can—"

"I may be out of here myself if things don't begin to work out better." She hadn't meant to say that! Libby put her hand over her mouth to try to recapture the words she had just allowed to escape from her lips. She was embarrassed that she had unburdened herself like that to a virtual stranger. Oddly, Greg did not seem like a stranger at all, but rather like an understanding friend. And the compassion she read in his eyes only intensified that feeling.

"I–I really must be going now." She rose to her feet and began edging toward the door. "Let me work on this for a few days, and I'll get back to you next week. I'm sure we can come to an understanding with your neighbors."

"Wait, Libby, don't rush off. Sit down and let's talk about this some more."

But Libby was already opening the front door. She felt an urgent need to get outside into the fresh air and get her thoughts in order. Why did this man's presence always seem to muddle her head so she came out with the most ridiculous words and ideas? She'd better leave before she blurted out another inane comment. "I'll think about this over the week-end and talk to you again next week."

"Bye, Miss Libby," Danny called out the door, as Libby hurried down the stairs.

seven

Tooling along the main drive in the Blue Dolphin golf cart, Libby headed toward the clubhouse. She wanted to check on the day's performance of the new cleaning service. Libby had recently finalized a contract with this new maintenance company, but the crew had been working on the premises for only six hours, and already she had received two complaints. One of the residents had called to complain that the soap dispenser in the ladies' lounge was empty, and another reported one of the trash cans in the card room had not been emptied. She thought it was probably only a matter of making sure the maintenance crew understood exactly what was expected.

"Hey, Miss Libby!" She looked up to see Danny trudging down the sidewalk toward home, swinging his lunch box in his hand.

"Hi, Danny. Hop in and I'll give you a lift to your building." Since building 300 was halfway between the front gate and the clubhouse, she'd be passing right by his parking lot.

Danny scrambled into the golf cart to sit beside her. "Gee, thanks! I'm really tired. I had a hard day today."

"Oh? What did you do today that was so tiring?" Libby tried hard not to allow her amusement to show.

"You know. Just the usual stuff. We had to read out loud, and then we had to add up some numbers, and learn about the weather and stuff. We're learnin' about different kinds of clouds. Then our art teacher came in and made us all draw pictures. Mine's not very good, but she hung it on the wall anyway."

"I'll bet it was *very* good. What kind of picture did you draw?"

"Just me and my dad in our boat, an' me pullin' in a big fish, but I couldn't draw my dad too good. I did better on the fish."

Libby swerved the golf cart into the parking lot of building 300. "Well, here's where you get off, Danny. I'd love to see that picture sometime."

Danny climbed out of the cart. "You would, Miss Libby? You really would?"

"Of course, Danny." Libby should have known better than to drop a casual remark to a child like Danny. His active little mind would expect her to follow up on it right away. "Stop by the office one day and show it to me after you're allowed to bring it home from school."

"No Ma'am, I can't do that. I don't reckon we're gonna get to bring 'em home. See, they're for our art show, but you could come there to my school and see it. Would you, Miss Libby, *please?*"

His soft, pleading eyes met hers with an urgency that was hard to resist. "I–I can't make you any promises, Danny. I'll have to see when it is. I have a lot to take care of here at Blue Dolphin, and. . .and at home too. I'm not sure I could get away."

"It's next Friday night at the school. I sure hope you can come, Miss Libby. We're supposed to bring our parents, but my dad can't come because he has a meeting with his boss that night. And, well, since I don't have a mom—"

Libby's heart sank like a lead weight. Poor little guy. "What time is the show, Danny?"

His face brightened, and his freckles seemed to sparkle on his chubby cheeks.

"Seven o'clock! I'll be lookin' for you. Wow! Wait'll I tell my teacher!" Danny made a dash toward the stairs but turned back to call over his shoulder, "Thanks, Miss Libby!"

"Wait, Danny, I didn't promise—" But her protest was lost in the wind, and she sighed as she added one more task to her mental list of things she must do before the weekend.

≥∎

On Friday evening, Libby pulled her Toyota into the parking lot of Longwood Elementary School. She found a space close to the front door. She had not talked to Danny about the art show since Monday afternoon when she had given him a ride in the golf cart, and she wondered if he even remembered he had invited her.

After finishing a quiet, simple supper at her kitchen table, Libby had longed to stay home with her sister and relax over a cup of hot tea. The idea of getting dressed and attending an art show did not hold much appeal for her, but the pleading green eyes of a motherless little boy kept prodding her conscience and eventually spurred her into action. Now in retrospect, she wondered if Celia might not have needed her more tonight than Danny. But she was here now. She would find Danny's classroom, admire his picture, and then hurry home to end the evening in the comfort of her living room.

Her heels made a clicking sound on the sidewalk as she followed a group of people toward the entrance. She heard a typical exchange of proud parental comments:

"My Heather painted a rainbow. Isn't that sweet? She's been so excited all week."

"Alex says he made a fire-breathing dinosaur. Isn't that just like a boy? We can't wait to see how he did it."

Inside the building, Libby wondered how she would find Danny's room. She hadn't even asked him the name of his teacher. "Excuse me," she asked one of the mothers, "could you tell me where the second-grade rooms are located?"

"Sure," came the friendly reply. "Right down this hall here. I'm Heather's mother. Whose mother are you?"

Libby swallowed. "I–I'm not a mother," she said. "Just a friend." But the lady was already moving down the hall at breakneck speed, so fast that Libby was sure she could not have heard her answer.

"Here we are." Heather's mother turned into a brightly lit room, and Libby followed.

An assortment of pictures was strung around three walls of the room, covering everything except the blackboard at the front of the class. Childish chatter permeated the air. "Look, Mama, here's mine!"

Libby let her eyes circle the room, searching for a curly red-haired little boy. Suddenly, from the back corner of the room, Danny's voice rose above all the rest of the noise. "You came! Miss Libby, you came!" He flung himself at her, his arms encircling her waist, and Libby steadied herself to keep from losing her balance. She had never seen such a show of emotion from Danny before. Her presence must mean more to him than she had realized, and suddenly she was very glad she had decided to come.

A female voice sounded over Libby's left shoulder. "Why, Danny, your mother did manage to come after all. I'm so glad."

Surprised, Libby turned to greet a tall, thin, bespectacled woman of about fifty. Libby hastened to explain, "Oh, I'm not—"

"This here's Miz Blackburn. Miz Joyner couldn't come tonight, so Miz Blackburn is takin' her place." Danny interrupted with his introduction so quickly that Libby did not have time to correct the teacher's error.

"I'm pleased you could come," Mrs. Blackburn said. "Mrs. Joyner's little girl is sick, so I agreed to fill in for her tonight. Danny's picture is right over there on the side wall. Take her over there and show her, Danny, and show her your reading workbook too."

Again Libby tried to explain her position to the teacher, but before she could get a word out of her mouth, a set of young parents had captured Mrs. Blackburn's attention and Danny began to pull her toward his picture.

"And you told me your picture wasn't good!" Libby chided, studying his artwork. "I think it's a great picture, Danny. I'm so glad you invited me to come by and see it. Now, I'm going to have to run along, but—"

"But you can't go yet," Danny protested, his eyes clouding up as he fought to hold back his tears. "We've been practicin' a song for you, and there's refreshments an' everything. It won't take long. Sit down over there, *please?*"

Libby noted that parents were claiming chairs that had been placed at the back of the room, and children were scampering off into another room for what was probably a final rehearsal before their "show."

What were a few more minutes, compared to breaking a little boy's heart? She took a seat in the last row, with an empty chair on either side of her. She checked her watch. She hoped Danny was right about the program being short. She really needed to get home and talk to Celia.

The crowd grew quieter now, in anticipation of the show that was about to begin. Mrs. Blackburn stood at the front of the room and prepared to make her announcement.

Heavy footsteps sounded in the doorway, and Libby was shocked to hear a low familiar voice. "Sorry I'm late, Mrs. Blackburn. I had a business meeting, but I decided to cut it short so I could come to see Danny's picture."

Greg! Libby felt light-headed and dizzy. She turned to look for a back door out of the room, but there was no escape.

"Why, come in, Mr. Cunningham." Mrs. Blackburn was shaking his hand. "You're just in time for our little show. Your wife is right back there in the last row. We're so glad you could come."

"My *what?*" Libby felt as though she were living her worst nightmare. She buried her head in her hands until she heard him say, "Oh, right. My wife. I'll just go back there and sit with her." Libby looked up in disbelief in time to see the wide grin that spread across Greg's face. Libby had never felt so mortified in her entire life.

Danny had plainly told her his father would not be able to come tonight. And why hadn't she corrected the teacher's initial mistake the moment she mistook Libby for Danny's mother? What had she gotten herself into? Now what was she going to do?

When he approached her chair, she stood. "Greg, please let me explain—"

"Shh!" The lady in front of her was obviously annoyed at the interruption of Libby's attempted conversation. The room had grown silent as the children filed into the room, spreading themselves across the front of the blackboard in perfect two-row formation.

Flashbulbs began to pop when the children began their song—something about a butterfly—but Libby could not concentrate on the words of the song. Greg's arm was pressed against hers, and the placement of the chairs made it impossible for her to put any distance between them. This had to be the most embarrassing moment of her entire life. As soon as the program was over, she would explain the whole situation to Greg, and then make her hasty departure.

The applause was deafening. She and Greg joined the others in clapping for the excited performers.

While a reporter from the local newspaper snapped pictures of the children, Mrs. Blackburn rapped on her desk to command the audience's attention. "Please feel free to look around at all the artwork of your talented children. And we have punch and cookies here on the front table."

Libby tried to sidle toward the exit, but Greg had a firm grip on her arm. "What's your hurry? We haven't looked at our little boy's picture yet." He pulled her toward the art displays.

"Greg, please let me explain." But at that precise moment, a flashbulb almost blinded her, and a reporter asked Greg, "Now, whose parents are you? I want to get all the names right for the *Star Journal*."

"I'm not—" Libby tried once more to explain, but Greg

beat her to the reply.

"Cunningham. We're here for Danny Cunningham." He offered a handshake, but the photographer was juggling his camera over his shoulder and his pad and pencil in his hands.

"Cunningham," he repeated. "Well, thank you, Mr. and Mrs. Cunningham. We run a weekly section on local school activities. Be sure to check in the Sunday edition of the *Star Journal*. It's too late for this weekend, but it'll probably run a week from Sunday. Let me get a close-up of your son's artwork." He aimed his camera at Danny's picture and snapped.

"Really, Greg. A joke is a joke, but this has gone far enough. I want you to straighten this whole thing out so I can leave."

Greg's grin had turned into a full-fledged chuckle. "What's to explain? Look at Danny. He's perfectly happy. Isn't that what you hoped to accomplish by coming here tonight?"

Danny pushed his way between them, cookie crumbs dripping from the corners of his mouth. "You made it, Dad! Isn't this great? Did you like the song? Did you see my picture, Dad?" Amid all this excitement, Libby knew any explanations would have to be put off until another day. Sometimes words only seemed to make matters more complicated than they were already, and the less said the better.

"It was a great evening, Danny. Thank you for inviting me." She patted the top of his curly hair. "I'll probably see you around Blue Dolphin tomorrow." She made her way to the front of the room where she hoped to have a parting word with Mrs. Blackburn and set the record straight, but the teacher was surrounded by a covey of proud parents. Libby eased her way through the door and down the hall.

"Wait, Libby." Greg's voice sounded from behind her, and she heard his footsteps running to catch her. Just outside the entry doors, he caught her at the top of the steps, and he was still grinning. How could he think this was funny? "Let me walk you to your car."

"That isn't necessary, Greg. I'm perfectly capable of—"

"Look, I'm sorry if I carried my joke a little too far. It's just that Mrs. Blackburn was so sure we were both Danny's parents, and it seemed easier to go along with that little misconception than to get into a detailed explanation of our relationship."

Relationship! There was no kind of relationship between them. Libby wished for a deep hole she could crawl into and hide. "Greg, I never gave that teacher any reason to believe I was Danny's mother. Believe me, this whole situation can be explained, but I can't talk about it tonight. I'm embarrassed and confused. And just suppose the *Star Journal* has my picture in it? Do you realize I could lose my job over a thing like this?"

For the first time that evening, the smile left Greg's face. "No! That's impossible! What possible concern could your employer have about a personal matter like this? It's certainly nobody's business but your own." He followed her down the steps and to her car. "Anyway, Libby, I doubt any of the residents of Blue Dolphin read the local elementary school news."

Standing in the shadows, he gripped both her arms. "Libby, the last thing in this world I would want to do is to make trouble for you. I know why you came here tonight, and believe me when I say I deeply appreciate your concern for Danny. You're just a very special kind of person."

Libby could feel hot tears pushing against her eyelids, struggling for release, and she blinked to force them back. The emotions of this night were just a climax to all that had troubled her life for the last few weeks—the insecurities of her job, her sister's health, the medical bills, and now this embarrassment—it was all just too much.

Greg's hands on her arms felt so strong and comforting. For a wild moment she had an impulse to lean her head against his chest and feel the warmth and security of his embrace. But instead, she pulled away from him and fumbled with her key in the lock of her car door.

"Here, let me do that for you." Greg took her key, unlocked her door, and held it open for her. "Please don't be upset about this evening, Libby. In a year or two, you'll be able to look back on this and laugh."

She could not trust herself to speak, certain that her voice would betray her fragile emotions. Without answering him, Libby closed her car door, shifted into reverse, and eased out of her parking space.

She doubted she would ever find any part of this night a matter to laugh about, but neither would she ever be able to forget even one single moment of it. Of that, she was absolutely certain.

eight

"There's a fresh pot of coffee," Lorraine said as Libby placed a stack of recently signed letters on her desk. "Now, I don't mean to be insulting, but you really do look like you could use a cup."

Libby was well aware of the dark circles shadowing her eyes. She had tried to cover them with makeup this morning, but nothing could disguise the lines of fatigue and worry brought on by recent weeks of sleepless nights and pressure-packed days. "Coffee sounds great, Lorraine. I'll help myself to a cup right now."

She poured a mug of the hot brew and returned to her own office. The board would be meeting again in just a few days, and if Libby was to be replaced by a new manager, she wanted to have everything in her office up-to-date and running like clockwork before he or she came onto the Blue Dolphin scene.

Michael had told her of the stormy stalemate at the first board meeting, and how this whole procedure was taking much longer than he had anticipated. The delay was taking its toll on Libby's nerves.

Would a new manager bring in his own assistant, or would Libby's services continue to be needed around here? As demeaning as it might feel to be demoted, Libby could not afford to leave her position at Blue Dolphin right now, no matter what alternative they offered her. With Celia's bills mounting, she'd have to take whatever she could get, at least until she had time to look around for something better.

Voices in the front office caught her attention, and she looked up. Through her partially open door, she could see

Michael Phillips talking with Selena and a young man whom she did not recognize. The three of them were bent over Lorraine's desk, speaking in lowered tones.

Libby left her desk and came through the doorway to greet them. "Good morning!"

"Oh, hi, Libby." Michael extended his hand and Libby responded with a firm shake. "Libby, this is Selena's nephew, Adam Ridgefield. He's visiting Selena, and he wanted to take a look around Blue Dolphin while he's in the area."

"Nice to meet you, Adam. Make yourself at home here. We're pretty proud of our complex." Libby acknowledged the introduction with a handshake, and noted that even Selena was smiling at her. Libby counted that as a good sign. Perhaps Selena was trying to forget their past differences and make amends. Libby was certainly willing to do her part by meeting her more than halfway. "Michael, would you like for me to give them the grand tour of the grounds in the golf cart?"

"Oh, no thanks, Libby," Michael answered, almost too quickly. "I can see you're busy. Go ahead with whatever you're doing. I'll just show them around a bit." Did Libby imagine it, or did Michael avert his eyes to avoid direct contact with hers? Was there more to this unexplained visit than she saw on the surface?

Libby returned to her own office, and this time she closed the door. She did not want to be accused of eavesdropping, even though in truth, she was fairly quivering with curiosity.

Her coffee had grown cold in the cup, and she no longer had the stomach for it anyway. She pulled up accounts receivable on her computer screen and poured her energy into delinquent maintenance payments. Most of the residents were prompt with their monthly payment, which covered water, sewer, garbage pickup, and cable television services, as well as ground maintenance and upkeep of all the Blue Dolphin amenities. But there were always a few, and generally the same few, who needed a gentle reminder each month. Usually that was the only action necessary; only rarely did she find it necessary to resort to legal procedures to collect the fees. Libby flagged the accounts that needed past due notices and printed out a list.

After a gentle knock on her door, Lorraine opened it a crack. "Aren't you going to break for lunch today?"

"Already?" Libby looked at her watch. "My, time flies when you're having fun," she quipped with a grin. "I have a few other things I want to finish first. Are you going out today, or did you bring your lunch?"

"I'm going to run over to my church for a quick one. The Women's Society is sponsoring a luncheon to raise money for missions. I won't be long. Want me to bring you a plate?"

"No thanks, Lorraine. For some reason, I'm not very hungry today. I may just skip lunch and eat after I get home. I want to check on Celia. Her appetite has slipped from very little to almost nothing. Please keep her in your prayers. I'm very worried about her."

"You know I will, Libby. Our prayer chain has her name on the list. I'm sure she's nervous about her upcoming surgery. As soon as that's over, I'm betting her appetite will improve."

"I hope so. Don't hurry back, Lorraine. I'll be here to answer the phone while you're gone. Take whatever time you need."

Lorraine grabbed her purse from the desk drawer and was almost out the door when Libby called to her. "By the way, Lorraine, what was that visit all about this morning? Do you have any idea?"

Lorraine took a deep breath. She walked a few steps back toward Libby's open door. "I wish you hadn't asked me that question. But you might as well know. You'll hear it soon enough anyway. Selena's nephew has just finished a course in property management at the junior college, and he's applying for a position here at Blue Dolphin."

"But that might be great news, Lorraine. Surely they wouldn't take someone right out of school, with no experience, and start him at the top." Libby pulled a pencil from behind her ear and twirled it thoughtfully. "Perhaps they're considering him for my old job as assistant manager. Oh, I suppose it might be awkward for me to work with one of Selena's relatives, but he seemed a pleasant enough fellow, and I can usually manage to get along with almost anyone if they give me half a chance."

"I hope that's what they have in mind," Lorraine said. But her tone implied she knew more about the situation than she had chosen to divulge, and Libby was intuitive enough to recognize the implication behind her unspoken words.

&

Greg rubbed his tired eyes and leaned back in his swivel chair. He had been at his drawing board all day without so much as a break, and he was beginning to see double. It was time for Danny to come home from school, so maybe he'd just hang it up for today and do something fun with his son.

He went to the kitchen and pulled a cola from the fridge. Popping the tab, he drank straight from the can. He looked out the window, and sure enough, there came Danny trudging across the tarmac, swinging his lunch box in his hand. Greg could only grin. What a terrific kid!

The art show at school had meant more to Danny than Greg had realized. And to think he had almost missed it. Only a last-minute decision convinced him to walk out on the meeting his boss had scheduled weeks in advance. Had he known Libby Malone planned to go, perhaps he would not have felt so guilty about missing the performance, but in retrospect, he was very glad he had gone.

Even so, the event had been a bittersweet experience for him. Seeing the interaction of so many happy family groups had made him realize anew just how much of life he was missing as a single parent. Maybe that was the reason he had so readily accepted Mrs. Blackburn's misconception of Libby Malone as his wife. He smiled, remembering how utterly sweet she had looked standing beside him.

Greg had long been praying that God would send a special person to round out his family and fill his house with love once more. But how was he to recognize her? Would God send him a sign? Recently he had wondered if Tiffany might be the woman whom God had chosen to be his lifetime companion, but last week's dinner had surfaced some serious doubts in his mind.

He tried to imagine Tiffany taking her place by his side at Danny's performance last Friday night, but the picture that filled his mind always turned into Libby Malone. There was something special about Libby—something that made Greg want to know more. What were her dreams and her goals? Was there a man in her life already, or was she an all-business, dyed-in-the-wool career woman? Perhaps he should give her a call and. . .

"Dad? I'm home!"

Greg's grin spread across his face, and all other thoughts were momentarily pushed aside. "Hiya, Pal. How about a glass of cold orange juice? Then maybe we'll wander down to the river and wet our fishing lines."

❧

When Michael Phillips returned to the administration building, he was alone. He walked past Lorraine's desk and went straight into Libby's office. "Hope I'm not interrupting anything."

"Of course not," Libby assured him. "In fact, I'm glad to see you. I wanted a chance to ask you about our office guest this morning. Was he favorably impressed with our condo community?"

Michael helped himself to a chair. "Well, you know Selena. She's never completely satisfied with anything. She noted some cracks in the sidewalks that need repair, and she wondered if the irrigation system was functioning properly. She pointed out a few dry spots in the grass."

Why wasn't Libby surprised that Selena only noticed all the problems and failed to comment on the improvements? "We have a company coming in on Thursday to repair the sidewalk cracks," she assured him. "I'm still trying to get the irrigation worked out. I've had lawn maintenance manually water a few troublesome spots until we can get everything up and running."

"Libby, you're doing a fine job. Personally, I have no complaints, but you might as well know that Selena is pushing me to give the position of manager to her nephew."

Libby paled. How could he even consider turning over a four hundred unit condominium community into the hands of someone with no experience at all?

"Selena is only one person, Libby. She shouldn't be able to control the whole board. But she has you under her microscope right now, so be sure you don't give her any reasons for legitimate complaint."

Libby remembered the day she had left work a few minutes early, only to have Selena come in and question Lorraine about her absence. "Is she still fussing about my leaving early that one afternoon?"

Michael shifted uneasily in his chair. "That, and. . ."

"Go ahead, Michael. And what?"

"Oh, it's too silly to mention. It seems she's seen you going into Lenore Cunningham's condo on two separate occasions, and she wondered if you and Mr. Cunningham were getting. . . um. . .chummy, that's all. I assured her you only went there on official Blue Dolphin business, but she was quick to tell me that that's what we have an office for."

Libby felt her cheeks burning. She could probably explain to Michael about the day Danny had spilled root beer all over her desk and clothes, and he would understand why she had scheduled the subsequent meeting away from the office. And she could easily explain about the other time when she went there to follow up on Mr. Kalinski's complaint. But Michael was already on her side, working to save her position. As for Selena, she would never understand Libby's explanations, simply because she did not want to.

"All I'm saying," Michael continued, "is that you must be careful to avoid anything that even gives the appearance of fraternization with a tenant, especially one who is young and attractive. Try not to worry, Libby. Just get on with your work, stick to business, and leave the worrying to me."

Beaming an encouraging smile, he rose to leave. Libby recognized and appreciated his futile attempts to ease her mounting tension. For his sake, she tried not to let them show.

"Thanks, Michael. You're a wonderful boss. I'll try to remember all the advice you've given me today and through the years." She smiled to mask her lingering anxieties and watched him walk away.

She was still pondering their conversation when her intercom buzzer sounded. "Yes, Lorraine?"

"Line two is for you. It's Mr. Cunningham."

"Thanks, I'll take it." With her finger hovering over the button to connect with her call, Libby took a deep breath. Her heart seemed to slide into a sudden tailspin. Why did the mere mention of this man's name produce such a volatile reaction in her? After all, Greg Cunningham was only one of hundreds of Blue Dolphin tenants. *Get a grip,* she warned herself. "Hello!"

"Is that you, Libby?"

"Yes, Greg. What is it? Do you have a problem?" Libby hoped the thunderous pounding of her heart could not be heard over the phone line.

"Oh, no. Nothing like that. I was just wondering—that is, Danny and I plan to ride out to the site this evening and see how our new house is progressing. I just wondered if you might like to go with us, just to see what we'll be moving into when we leave here?"

Libby could think of nothing she'd like better, but as much as she longed to accept his invitation, Michael's words were still ringing in her ears. *No fraternization with the tenants!* She hesitated for a few moments. Shouldn't her after-hours time be her own? "Well, I. . . "

"We could stop for dinner at that new Chinese restaurant downtown before we come back."

He was making it very difficult for her to refuse, but Libby simply could not afford to ignore the Four Star policy, especially at this tenuous time. She couldn't risk losing her job over this. "Greg, as much as I'd like to, um. . .I'm afraid Michael wouldn't approve, and you see, he's my—"

Greg cut her reply short. "I understand, Libby. It's okay."

Libby realized he had completely misunderstood her refusal. She tried again to explain. "I'd love to go, Greg. I really would. But right now especially, I have to do things Michael's way, because he's the—"

"Never mind, Libby. I certainly wouldn't want to do anything to offend *Michael*." The edge in his voice was as sharp as a freshly honed knife. "Gotta go now. I'll see you around."

Libby sat holding a dead line. He had actually hung up on her! That was just plain rude! She had never before known anyone like Greg Cunningham. How could she continue to feel any attraction at all to such an overbearing man?

He had not even given her time to explain that Michael Phillips was the president of Four Star Management Company, and that her job security rested in his hands. Just what was Greg thinking when he ended their conversation so abruptly? Well, she'd never know, because she wasn't going to waste any more time worrying about someone without the common courtesy to hear her out! Her hand was trembling when she replaced the receiver on its cradle.

❧

Greg knew he had blown it. But when Libby had burst his balloon by telling him that her destiny was linked to some man named Michael, Greg's spirits crumbled like a bag of crushed cookies.

It had taken him all afternoon to work up the courage to call and ask her to go out with him. He had practiced two or three different approaches, trying to make sure he didn't come on too strong, but in the end, it wouldn't have mattered. Nothing would have made any difference. Who was this Michael guy anyway, that Libby would allow him to dictate her every move? He must be very important to her, but he had credited her with more independence than that.

But he should not have hung up on her; he knew better than that. If he had talked to her longer, maybe he could have learned the answer to his question, and a few others that kept nagging his mind.

He slammed his fist hard against the desk. He was not a violent man, but he had suddenly developed a passionate dislike for a man he did not even know. He just hoped that Michael, whoever he was, was deserving of all that loyalty from a girl as special as Libby Malone.

nine

Celia's operation was set for early Wednesday morning. She would be admitted into Martin Memorial Hospital at six A.M. so she could be prepped and ready for surgery by seven-thirty. Celia seemed much calmer about the whole ordeal than Libby.

"Are you sure you packed everything you need in your overnight case?" Libby asked, standing beside her sister at the admissions desk.

"Yes, Silly. What could I possibly need besides my comb and toothbrush? They'll dress me in one of those stylish hospital gowns that are split up the back, and I'll probably be ready to go home by tomorrow afternoon."

The biopsy was to be performed while Celia was still under the anesthetic, and a decision would be made as to the necessity and extent of further surgery. This was a possibility the two sisters discussed as little as possible.

"I'll be here every minute, waiting for your doctor to come out and give me his report," Libby told her.

"Are you sure this isn't going to make any problems for you at work?" Celia asked. "I know how much they depend on you to be there now that Jake is gone."

"It's all arranged. I'm taking a day of my vacation leave—more if necessary—to stay with you until this is over. Pastor Redding has promised to be here with me too. He said the church members have already started a twenty-four hour prayer chain that will continue until you have fully recovered."

"I'm so glad he's going to be with you today, Libby. You need him more than I do. I wish you would calm down and quit worrying about me. Dr. Jennings referred me to the man he considers to be the best surgeon on the staff—a Dr. Shaeffer."

"Dr. Jennings has certainly gone the extra mile to see that you get the kind of attention you should have, Celia. I can tell he really cares about you."

"Yes, he's a fine Christian doctor. He even took time to pray with me on my last visit. Not many doctors would do that. We all know I'm in the Lord's hands, and now we must all have faith that everything is going to turn out just fine!"

Libby listened to Celia's words of comfort and thought it ironic that Celia was once again the caregiver, and she the recipient of her sister's kindness and consideration. Wasn't that the way it had always been? *Oh, Lord,* she prayed, *please bless and take care of my sister Celia. I can't imagine a life without her.*

"Right this way, Miss Malone. Follow me, please." A nurse led the way down a wide corridor, and both sisters fell in line behind her. Hearing the extra set of footsteps, the nurse turned back and addressed her words to Libby. "I'm afraid you'll have to wait up front. As soon as we have your sister settled in her room, you may stop in for a short visit, but we'll be giving her something to help her relax. You'll have to wait in the lounge, but we'll come out and give you a report as soon as the surgery is over. You'll have plenty of time to get some coffee in the cafeteria now, if you'd like."

"Yes, Libby," Celia urged her. "Go have a good breakfast in the cafeteria. It's terrible you had to be dragged out of bed this morning before the sun was up. Now, try not to worry. I'm in good hands." She put her arms around Libby and kissed her. "Now, be a good girl and scoot." She gave her a playful swat on the behind, just as she might have done fifteen years earlier.

Libby's gaze followed them as the nurse led Celia down the hall, and neither of them turned back to see the lady standing alone, with tears streaming down her cheeks.

ಶಿ

When Greg checked his mailbox on Wednesday, he was
pleased to find a letter from his mother. She was due to come
home soon, and he was looking forward to seeing her again.
She'd be surprised at how much Danny had grown over the
summer.

Although Greg frequently talked to his mother on the telephone, Lenore Cunningham had nurtured a love of letter
writing for as long as he could remember. She faithfully kept
in touch with friends she had not seen in years, using only
the finest stationery and pens to pursue her hobby, and Greg
could always count on at least one letter a week.

He took his mail and went back upstairs to his condo before
he ripped open the thin pink envelope. It smelled of lavender
and brought a pleasant flush of nostalgia to his mind.

As he read the words, he could almost hear his mother's
voice.

Dearest Greg,

*I will be driving out of here next Friday, and if all
goes well, I should arrive at my home in Florida on
Monday or Tuesday of next week. I'll stop overnight at
your sister's house in Virginia, and unless she talks me
into staying an extra night, I'll make it the rest of the
way home by Monday. I'll try to work out an itinerary
for my nightly stops while I'm at Patty's house, and
leave it with her in case you need to contact me before I
get home.*

*I'm so eager to get back and see you and Danny
again. How is work progressing on the new house? Dare
I hope it is delayed so that I can have you two as my
guests a little longer?*

*Tell Danny I am bringing him a little surprise. And
Greg, I may have a surprise for you as well. Do you
remember my friend, Gladys? Well, she told me that her*

*niece has just moved to Florida, and she wants me to get
the two of you together. I may plan a little dinner one
evening. Wouldn't that be nice?*

*Don't worry about getting everything in the condo
cleaned up for my return. I'll see to everything once I
get back.*

Your loving mother

Greg folded the two delicate sheets of stationery and
placed them back into their envelope. He chuckled aloud.
His mother was determined to end his bachelor days, and no
amount of persuasion could get her to let up on him. Maybe
he should hint that he had already found someone, just to
get her off his back. He'd give that some thought. But of
course, she would immediately insist on meeting the lady of
his choice, and worse than that, she'd probably throw a lav-
ish dinner party to celebrate. No, he'd better think of something else.

One thing he'd have to do, in spite of his mother's words
to the contrary, would be to clean out the refrigerator and get
the place spruced up a bit. He wanted to leave it like they
found it when they came. He and Danny kept things pretty
well organized on the surface, but they would have to spend
the whole weekend doing some serious cleaning before
Lenore Cunningham returned.

≈

Libby sat in the waiting room and chewed her fingernails, a
habit she had never indulged in before today. How long
would she have to wait for the surgeon to come out and give
his report?

"Isn't this taking an unusually long time?" she asked Pastor
Redding.

The kind minister patted her hand. "I don't think so, Libby.
These things take time. You wouldn't want the doctors to
hurry, would you?"

"No, I suppose not, but it seems to me they've had plenty of time by now. Do you think they might have encountered a problem?"

"Now, Libby, you mustn't assume the worst. Dr. Shaeffer explained to you that they planned to do a biopsy during the surgery, and that they won't be able to give us a full report until all of that is out of the way. Your sister put herself in God's hands, and you must do the same. Would you like us to pray again?"

But before Libby could answer him, Dr. Shaeffer, still wearing his scrubs, stepped into the waiting room, and Dr. Jennings was with him. Libby jumped up to meet them at the door. "How is she, Doctor? Is everything all right?"

"Your sister is going to be just fine, Miss Malone. We removed the tumor, which I am happy to report proved to be benign. She'll probably be ready to go home in a few days."

"And you're sure she's fine?" Libby felt dizzy with relief. Her prayers had been answered, and Celia was fine!

"Hold on, little lady. I didn't say she *is* fine," the doctor corrected. "I said she's *going* to be fine. Miss Malone, I don't know what kind of life your sister has been leading, but she is extremely run down. We've given her a blood transfusion to raise her red cell count. Dr. Jennings will be discussing a diet and exercise program with your sister, but the most important thing right now is for her to get lots of rest and eat regular, well-balanced meals. If she doesn't follow those instructions, she is going to end up right back here in the hospital, and next time the outlook might not be so optimistic."

Libby's spirits, so high only moments ago, now took a dive. "I'll see that she does everything the way she's supposed to, Dr. Shaeffer." The last thing either she or Celia wanted was for Celia to have to return to the hospital. "Oh, and thank you for everything, Doctor. When will I be able to see her?"

"She's in recovery right now. The nurses will be moving her into her room in about an hour, and you may visit her for a few moments then. But remember everything I've told you, and try not to tire her. I'm going to limit her visitors for a few days to her pastor and her immediate family. She tells me that is only you."

"Yes. Well, we'll only stay for a little while, and then we'll go home and let her rest. I just need to see her for my own peace of mind. Thank you, Doctor. And thank you too, Dr. Jennings, for standing by. I know Celia appreciates that."

Pastor Redding stood beside Libby, steadying her with a hand on her elbow. "We have a little time before we can visit Celia. Let's go into the hospital chapel and thank God for all the blessings of this day," he suggested.

"Yes, and we'll ask Him to strengthen Celia and restore her to good health."

✿

It frightened Libby to see her sister so still and pale against the stark white hospital sheets. "Celia?"

Celia's eyelids fluttered and she gave Libby a weak smile. "Good news," she whispered. "I'll soon be good as new, up and running again."

Libby did not argue with her sister now—the arguments would come much later. She had no doubt there would be a major protest when she insisted that Celia take a long vacation from her job at the café.

Celia would remind her of the mounting medical bills and the high cost of living. Well, the bills would just have to be paid little by little, and somehow they would manage to get by on Libby's salary alone. She was not going to let Celia go back to work at that café, even if she had to tie her to the bedpost to keep her home!

"Libby, don't try to come to the hospital tomorrow," Celia pleaded. "I'll be taken care of by the nurses, and you need to take care of your responsibilities at work."

Libby could see that each word was an effort for Celia, so she did not challenge her decision. "All right, Honey. But I'll see you tomorrow after work. And you have my phone number at Blue Dolphin in case you need anything. I'll be calling during the day to check on your progress."

Celia answered with a fragile smile.

Pastor Redding placed his hand on Celia's arm, being careful not to disturb the IV tube that dripped glucose into her vein. "We're so thankful your surgery turned out to be uncomplicated. Now we just want you to rest and regain your strength, Celia, so we're going to leave now, and let you go back to sleep."

Libby could tell by the sound of her shallow, steady breathing that her sister had indeed already gone back to sleep.

She and the pastor slipped quietly out of the room and headed down the hall toward the elevators. Libby was so tired that she ached, but she felt at least one of her burdens had been lifted from her shoulders. What she needed now was a nice warm bath and a peaceful night's sleep. She had much to be thankful for this day. Tomorrow she would be ready to face the world again.

ten

"Did anything unusual take place in my absence yesterday, Lorraine, or was it just an ordinary Wednesday?" Libby used one hand to flip through the stack of mail piled on her desk, using the other to hold the telephone receiver while she talked with her secretary over the intercom.

"Nothing except that the phone rang all day long. You know how fast news flies through the condo grapevine. There must have been fifty people who called in and asked about Celia's surgery, and all of them seemed sincerely concerned. Sometimes we don't realize how many friends we have until we run into a problem. You had all kinds of offers of help, but most of the callers simply wanted you to know they were praying for both you and your sister. You have a lot of people out here who love you, Libby."

"That's truly heartwarming, Lorraine. I'll be sure to tell all this to Celia when I visit her tonight. She's been worried about my taking the time off work all day yesterday to be with her, but of course I couldn't do anything else."

"Well, you can both quit worrying about that. Everything ran smoothly. Even Michael Phillips called to get a midday report on Celia, and sent word to you to take whatever time you needed."

"Michael is a caring employer, isn't he? I honestly believe he is trying his hardest to see that I get to stay on here in the manager's seat."

"He is, Libby. I know he is. He puts in a good word for you every chance he gets. And surely it would be a lot easier on him to keep you in place than it would be to train a new manager who wouldn't know beans about the workings of Blue Dolphin."

"It would seem so." Libby's wistful comment sounded less than confident. Then, hearing the other phone line chime, Libby whispered a hasty, "Talk to you later." She replaced her receiver so Lorraine could answer the call and get on with her work in the front office. Libby had plenty of catching up to do herself after being out all day yesterday. She grabbed her letter opener and slit the first envelope on the top of the stack.

Even as she worked, Libby continued to lift her thoughts in praise and thanksgiving to the Lord for all the blessings He had heaped into her life this past week. She made a silent vow to try harder to focus her attention on her many blessings instead of ruminating on her troubles. Celia was right. Whenever she placed herself into the hands of her Lord, everything worked out for the best.

By three o'clock, Libby had cleared her desk of paperwork and decided to take the cart down to the clubhouse. She liked to check on the pool and tennis court area at least every other day.

She was just climbing into the golf cart when she heard the squeaking wheels of the school bus. Danny would be coming in from school. She'd wait by the gate and give him a ride as far as his parking area.

She could hardly suppress a chuckle as she watched him start down the sidewalk toward home. He turned back once to wave good-bye to his friends on the bus. Both his shoes were untied, their laces dragging in the dirt; his shirttail hung outside his baggy jeans; and his hair, like always, looked as though it had been combed with an eggbeater.

"Hi, Danny. Want a ride?"

His widespread grin took the place of an answer as he ran to catch up with her. "Wow, thanks. I can sure use a lift." He puckered his lips and exhaled, as though he had been digging ditches all day.

"Another tough day, huh?"

"Yeah, an' I've just got a lot on my mind these days. Lots of problems."

Libby tried to make her voice sound sober enough to match his mood. It wouldn't do to laugh at him or make light of his perceived problems. "Well, you'll soon be home, and then maybe you can rest and take it easy."

"Not for long. Me and Dad have to go out and check on the new house again. They was supposed to get the inside doors hung today. I sure hope they get a good solid one on my room, with a lock too, so Tiffany won't go nosin' around in there. See, that's part of my problems."

Taken by surprise, Libby's foot accidentally slipped off the accelerator, and the cart jerked before she regained her footing. "Tiffany?"

"Yeah, I think she an' my dad are fixin' to get married when the house is finished." Danny's tone left no doubt that this idea was not to his liking.

"I–I didn't know your father was engaged to be married, Danny. When is this. . .um. . .event going to take place?" Today, tomorrow, or next year. Why did it matter an iota to her? It was certainly nothing to her one way or another. She was simply expressing a polite interest in Danny's welfare, because he was such a sweet little boy.

"I dunno when," Danny admitted. "They never tell me anything, but I can figure out a lot of things for myself. I'm a lot smarter than they think I am."

"I believe that may be true," Libby agreed cautiously. "Well, here's your building, Danny. I enjoyed talking to you again. Stop in and see me anytime you feel the need for someone to talk to. I'm almost always around here somewhere." She waited while he collected his belongings and prepared to climb out of the cart.

Before his feet hit the ground, he turned back and gave Libby a long hard stare. "Mind if I ask you a kinda personal question, Miss Libby?"

Libby rolled her eyes heavenward and sent up a quick prayer for wisdom. She never knew what to expect next from this child. "Well, you can ask, and then I'll decide about whether or not I want to answer."

"Well, I was just wonderin'. . ." Danny lowered his gaze for one thoughtful moment before connecting again with her eyes. "Do you have a boyfriend?"

Libby felt heat rising to her cheeks. "A boyfriend? You mean like—a steady one?" She wondered if Danny could tell she was stalling for time. She realized now that this innocent little boy had developed a romantic crush on her, which was very flattering, and too, it explained a lot about his many probing questions and stares. While she was reluctant to encourage his fantasies, at the same time, she did not want to throw cold water on his childish dreams. She remembered such dreams herself when she was much younger. At Danny's age, she had been madly in love with John Travolta, and she knew firsthand how tender and fragile first love could be.

Danny's piercing, relentless gaze told her he would not let go of his question until he had received his answer. She proceeded with caution. "Uh, no, I don't have a real boyfriend. I guess you could say I have lots of friends, both men and women, but not one special one. Does that answer your question?"

Danny looked more than pleased with her reply. In fact, he looked simply ecstatic. He gave a whoop as he jumped from the cart and turned back to wave at her. "Thanks for the ride, Miss Libby. An' thanks for invitin' me to stop by to visit you. I'll come by real soon, okay?"

"Sure, Danny. Take care." Libby could chuckle now that he was out of earshot. It appeared she now had a new admirer.

Libby removed her foot from the brake, and the golf cart seemed to take on a life of its own, following the curving path of Dolphin Drive. Her thoughts followed their own curving path, veering between her sister's hospital room, an upcoming wedding, and a small boy whose problems—however small in reality—seemed monumental to the mind of a seven year old.

&

From his upstairs window, Greg easily spotted his son's red head perched beside Libby in the golf cart. Transfixed to the spot, he continued to watch, observing that the two appeared to be in serious conversation. What was Danny cooking up with the pretty property manager this time? Surely not another invitation to attend one of his school functions! Greg laughed in spite of himself, remembering the farce his son had created with that last invitation.

It was evident to Greg that Danny had a colossal crush on the brown-eyed lady with the golden hair, which only went to prove his son had excellent taste in women. Not only was Libby drop-dead gorgeous, she was one of the kindest, gentlest women he had ever been privileged to meet, with a depth of character that went far beneath the surface of her outer beauty.

Yes, Danny could not have chosen a better recipient of his first love. In fact, if it were not for this Michael guy—whoever he was—Greg might be tempted to give his son some friendly competition in the category of love.

He'd like to meet that Michael-what's-his-name, just to size up what kind of fellow could get such a strong hold on an independent woman like Libby. Who was it who said, "All is fair in love and war?" Greg had never run from good, healthy competition. Perhaps a little rivalry for the attention of Libby Malone might not be out of order after all.

eleven

Libby steered her cart into the parking lot adjacent to the clubhouse, removed the key from the ignition, and followed the sidewalk into the recreational complex.

All four of the tennis courts were in use, and the swimming pool was crowded with people enjoying the balmy days of early autumn. While northern states were reporting snowfall three feet deep, here in south Florida the temperature was a comfortable 70 degrees. Libby felt blessed to live and work in such a pleasant place.

She stood by the edge of the pool and dipped her fingers into the warm water. Satisfied the thermostat was functioning properly, she turned to walk away.

"Libby," one of the swimmers called. "How is your sister?"

Libby turned to acknowledge the white-haired lady who voiced her concern. "I called the hospital right after lunch today, and the nurse told me her condition was stable. She was sleeping when I called, so I didn't get to talk to her, but I'll be going to see her as soon as I leave here today. I'll be sure to tell her you asked about her. Thank you, Mrs. Rollins."

By now, several people had clustered around to add their good wishes for Celia's speedy recovery. "We all have her in our prayers," one man assured her. "Now, you try not to worry too much, because your sister is going to be just fine."

"Thank you, Mr. McIntyre. Thanks to all of you for your good wishes, and especially for your prayers. They mean so much to both of us."

Libby gave a cursory glance at the tennis courts and acknowledged several waves. She entered the clubhouse through the back door and observed an aerobics class in progress. Just as Lorraine had said, everything at Blue Dolphin seemed to be running smoothly. If only she could keep it that way, without any undue emergencies, at least until a decision had been reached about her job! She wondered how long she would have to wait for an answer from Michael Phillips. For now, the matter was entirely out of her hands. She renewed her determination to put that concern out of her mind and concentrate her efforts on doing the best job possible—not only to enhance her chances of continuing on as on-site manager of Blue Dolphin, but to fulfill her personal commitment to all the people who lived here. They were like a big warm family to her, even though, like other families, they had their disagreements from time to time. She made a silent vow to offer them her best for as long as she was allowed to act as their manager.

She reclaimed the golf cart from the parking lot and began the drive back down the road toward the administration building. It would soon be time to clean off her desk and get over to the hospital for a visit with Celia. She prayed she would find her sister much stronger today.

Passing building 300, she could not resist a glance at the parking lot, where Danny and Greg were just backing their Wrangler out of the carport. No doubt they were on their way to inspect the new house. Would Tiffany be there to join them? Not if Danny had any say in the matter, but Libby doubted that he did. His earlier words rang in her ears. *They never tell me anything!*

She was glad she had invited the little boy to stop into her office for a visit. It was plain that he longed for someone in whom he could confide. Celia had always been the one there for Libby, to provide a steadying influence all through her growing years. Now perhaps she could give back a little of that through her friendship with Danny.

Last Tuesday when Greg had invited her to ride out with him and see his new house, she had refused out of allegiance to Michael Phillips and his rule that Four Star Management employees were not to fraternize with the residents. In retrospect, she had begun to regret that decision, rationalizing she would not have taken any time away from her working hours. What she did with her free time should not be anyone's business but her own, should it?

At the time, she had been annoyed with Greg, because she had interpreted his abrupt end to their conversation as an act of rudeness. But later she thought she might have been unfair. It was just possible he could have accidentally dropped the receiver, or perhaps there was another emergency with Danny that demanded his immediate attention. Such emergencies seemed to occur with enough regularity to be considered a normal part of his daily routine. She decided that if Greg called and invited her again, she would seriously consider going along to see his new home.

But with the revelation of his impending marriage to Tiffany, Libby could only be thankful she had resisted the impulse to accept his invitation. She realized now that he had simply been acting out of appreciation for her attention to Danny. There could not have been any personal design on his part, and she might have come off looking like a fool again. How fortunate that she had found out in time to avoid yet another embarrassing episode involving Greg Cunningham!

ও

Celia was propped up in bed, pretty in the new pink bed jacket that Libby had bought as a gift before her surgery. Her well-worn leather Bible was cradled in her hands. Soft brown hair was tied back from her face with a pink satin ribbon, and several floral arrangements brightened her room.

"My goodness, don't you look like the princess?" Libby crooned. "I hope you don't get too spoiled with all this attention. Who are the flowers from?"

"The ones in the window are from all my friends at the café, and ones on the dresser are from your boss, Michael

Phillips. The rosebuds here by my bed are from Dr. Jennings. They're all lovely, aren't they? I certainly never expected anything like this."

"Well, you deserve all of it and more, Celia. I'm touched that Michael Phillips sent flowers. He really is a caring person. But I'm a little surprised that your doctor would send flowers. I've never heard of that custom. Do the doctors do that nowadays for all their patients?"

Celia's pale cheeks showed a faint tinge of pink. "I–I don't really know. But it was very thoughtful of him, wasn't it?"

Libby nodded and placed a warm kiss on her sister's forehead. She glanced at the card attached to the rosebuds, and read just one simply scrawled word: "Bob."

"I'm so glad you're stronger today, Celia. I'm happy to see they've removed your IV tube. Those things must be pretty uncomfortable. Are you eating regular meals now?"

"I haven't developed much of an appetite yet, but I'm trying. Dr. Jennings says I should gain a few pounds, so I'm really going to work on that."

"I suppose they've had you up and walking around already," Libby surmised.

"Well, no, not yet. It seems I developed a blood clot in my left leg, and Dr. Jennings wants to be sure it's completely dissolved before I get up. I sure hope it's okay soon, though, because I don't want to stay here in the hospital even one day longer than is absolutely necessary. Just imagine what my bill must be already!"

"We aren't going to worry about things like that right now, Celia," Libby admonished, hands on hips for added emphasis. "I just want you to have everything you need to restore you to good health. We can talk about money later, but all the money in the world can't buy me a new sister. Besides, I'm pretty fond of the one I have already." She leaned over and squeezed Celia's hand and noted the moisture glistening in her sister's eyes.

Libby found a straight chair under the window and moved it closer to the bed so she could continue to hold Celia's hand while they talked. Determined to keep the conversation on a happy note, Libby tried to think of all the amusing things that had happened at work during the day. She told her of the many people who had called to inquire about her surgery, and of the well-wishers she had encountered at the swimming pool. "Everyone sends love and prayers for your speedy recovery."

"How sweet. I'm glad you have such a pleasant place to work, Libby, even though I know you still must miss Jake terribly. I thank God every day that He has given you the opportunity to work among such wonderful people."

Most of them really are, Libby thought. But as the old adage goes, It only takes one bad apple to spoil the barrel. She thought of Selena and a few of the other residents who were determined to see her replaced, but she carefully avoided any mention of her present worries. Instead, she tried to think of something that would bring a smile to Celia's face.

"Remember the little boy I told you about—the one who spread terror in the clubhouse one day by releasing his pet frog?"

Celia's chuckle was a delightful sound to Libby's ears. "Yes, I remember. Isn't he the same one who spilled root beer all over your desk and clothes?"

"That's the one," Libby said. "Well, now it seems he has a romantic crush on me. Can you imagine that? Looks like I've got me a new boyfriend."

Celia's amusement exploded into full-blown laughter. "Can't you do better than that, little sister? Aren't there any good-looking men over seven and under seventy out there where you work?"

Libby laughed too, but for some inexplicable reason, the sudden image of Greg Cunningham popped into her mind, and the laughter died on her lips. Spluttering to return to a safer area of conversation, she stammered, "I—he—the little boy is really rather sweet. I'm becoming fond of him in spite of his mischievous nature."

Celia raised a questioning eyebrow, but Libby was spared further interrogation by a knock on the partially closed door.

Without waiting for an invitation, Dr. Jennings entered the room. "What's going on in here?" he asked with a broad smile. "I thought I ordered rest for this patient, but it sounds like she's having a party."

"No, nothing like that," Libby assured him. "We're just catching up on some girl talk."

"My little sister is the best tonic you could possibly prescribe for me, Dr. Jennings. I hope you aren't going to order her to leave."

"No, of course I'm not," he said. "I just happened to be in the neighborhood, so I thought I'd stop in and see how my star patient is doing. From the sound of things, I'd say she is improving by leaps and bounds." He reached for Celia's wrist and checked her pulse. "I've ordered a nutritional shake for you to drink before you go to sleep tonight. I want you to be sure to finish all of it. In fact, I may drop back in here later on, just to make sure that you do." He squeezed her hand and edged toward the door. "You two go ahead with your girl talk, but absolutely no dancing!" he quipped before disappearing through the doorway.

"He certainly seems to be the most caring doctor I've seen in a long time," Libby mused. "He must be very busy if he gives all his patients this much attention."

Celia smiled. "Yes. Yes, I'm sure he's very busy. Now, finish telling me about this little boy who has a crush on you. How are you going to handle it?"

Libby did not resist Celia's obvious efforts to change the subject of their conversation, and she had not missed the heightened color in her sister's cheeks the moment the good doctor entered the room. *Hmm!*

Heavy wheels sounded in the corridor and came to a halt

just outside Celia's door. "Suppertime!" A smiling aide delivered a large tray, its contents mysteriously hidden by an assortment of stainless steel covers. Adjusting the bedside table so that it slipped over Celia's knees, the young woman asked, "Would you like to have your head raised a little more, Miss Malone?"

"Supper already?" Celia's eyebrows arched like two half-moons. "I thought I had just finished lunch." She lifted the lid off one of the plates and heaved a heavy sigh of resignation. "Yes, I guess I do need to have my bed adjusted a little."

The aide cranked Celia into an upright position. "I'll be back for your tray in a little while. Enjoy!" On rubber-soled shoes, she slipped out of the room while Celia continued to lift the lids and inspect her food. "Thanks!" she remembered to call to the retreating aide.

"Beef tips over rice, tossed salad, lima beans, and a scrumptious-looking dessert. That looks wonderful!" Libby observed, leaning over to give her approval to the meal.

"Let me ring for the nurse and see if we can order a guest tray for you," Celia suggested. "Then we can enjoy our supper together."

"No, I need a shower first. I'll just grab a quick bite when I get back to the house. But I think I'll run along now and let you eat in peace. The smell of all that food has just reminded me that I haven't stopped to eat since breakfast, and all of a sudden I'm famished!"

Libby bent across the tray of food to give her sister a kiss on the cheek. "Do everything they tell you, Honey, so we can get you out of this place and back home where you belong. I'll be back to see you again tomorrow. Maybe by then the good doctor will give us a release date."

"I'll ask him next time he comes in," Celia said. "Be careful going home, Libby, and call me as soon as you get there."

"Will do," Libby promised as she picked up her purse. She blew Celia one last kiss, then disappeared beyond the door.

twelve

After Danny left to catch the school bus on Friday morning, Greg decided to use the hours of his son's absence to catch up on a few errands that needed last-minute attention before he moved over to his new house on Saturday. He gathered his dry cleaning into a pile on the couch and stacked his outgoing mail on the table.

He pulled his checkbook from the desk drawer and wrote a check to Blue Dolphin Condominium Association to cover his monthly maintenance fees, realizing that this would be his last month in residence before moving into his new home. As much as he had looked forward to living in his own place, Greg was now beginning to experience some mixed emotions he was clueless to explain. He should be wildly happy. At last he would be done with all these endless condominium rules and restrictions, done with nosy neighbors, done with cramped working conditions, and done with—*Libby Malone!* Why that should bother him so much he could not imagine— she had caused him nothing but trouble. And she had made it very clear her interests were centered on a guy named Michael. Yet there was something about her that kept seeping into his thoughts, causing a surge of adrenaline through his system at the mere mention of her name.

Danny too seemed to be attracted to Libby. The two hit it off like bread and jam. More than once, Greg had felt a twinge of envy just watching the two of them together.

Well, it wasn't as though he had not tried to know her better. He had even invited her to go out with him once, but she had cut him short with a reference to this Michael guy. He might as well wipe all thoughts of Libby Malone from his mind. He certainly wasn't going to bow down and have his nose rubbed in the dirt.

He started to address an envelope for the check he had just written, but stopped when he had a sudden inspiration. Why mail his payment when he would be driving right by the administration building in a few minutes? Why not drop in and hand the check to Libby in person? Cheered by that thought and forgetting his resolve of only moments ago, he changed his shirt, brushed his teeth for the second time since breakfast, and ran a comb through his thick dark hair.

He arrived at the administration office at eight forty-five. Already several cars had claimed the prime spaces in front of the building, and Greg was forced to park half a block away. He had expected the office would be almost empty at this early hour, except for the staff, of course.

He twisted the knob of the front office door, pushed it open and stepped inside. Lorraine, the secretary, greeted him cheerfully. "Come in, Mr. Cunningham. How can I help you?"

Greg eyed a small group of people standing in the middle of the room, apparently in serious conversation. He recognized Selena Watson and wondered what trouble she was cooking up this time. He did not know either of the two men with her.

The check in his hand could easily have been handed over to Lorraine. In fact, that would be the normal thing to do. He hesitated, letting his gaze slip to the closed door of Libby's office.

Lorraine tried once more. "Mr. Cunningham, can I do something for you? Or did you need to speak to Libby?"

"No, I—yes. Yes, I would like to speak to Libby if she's available." Now that he had asked for her, what was he going to say that would make any sense at all?

Lorraine pushed a button on the intercom. "Libby, Mr. Cunningham is in the front office. He'd like to speak to you if you have a moment. Shall I send him in?"

When she replaced the receiver, she raised her eyes to meet Greg's. "She's going to step out here and talk to you in just a minute. Would you like to sit down over there while you wait?"

"No thanks, I'll just stand." Greg walked over to the window and watched two squirrels chase each other across the grass. He could not help but wonder at the serious discussion taking place in the center of the room, but lowered voices prevented the satisfaction of his curiosity.

When the inner office door opened, all attention turned to Libby. "Good morning, all," she said, forcing cheer into her voice. "Have all of you met?"

When she didn't receive an immediate answer, she continued talking to cover up the awkward silence. "Selena, I believe you know Greg Cunningham. . ."

"Yes, we've met," Selena acknowledged through tight lips.

"And Greg, have you met Selena's nephew, Adam Ridgefield. . .?"

Greg repeated the name as the two of them shook hands, "Adam. . ."

"And this is my boss, Michael Phillips, the owner of Four Star Property Managers."

Greg reached to meet Michael's outstretched hand. "Michael. How do you do?" Then, as if a lightbulb clicked on in Greg's mind, he grabbed Michael's hand again, giving it a hearty shake. "Oh, *you're* Michael." So this was Libby's Michael! The gentleman must have been at least sixty years old, and he was Libby's employer. That began to clear up a lot of things. Greg pumped the man's hand until Michael Phillips finally drew away from his grip. "I'm very happy to meet you," Greg said with an enthusiasm that brought a look of astonishment to the group surrounding him.

Libby, who seemed as perplexed as the others, nevertheless rescued the tense situation. "You wanted to see me, Greg? Is there a problem?"

"Problem? No, not at all. Absolutely no problem. I just wanted to give you this." He held out the crumpled check he had been carrying since he left home. "It's. . .it's my maintenance fee for the month."

Libby gave him a puzzled look, but she accepted his check and handed it to Lorraine. "Thank you, Greg. Was there anything else?"

"No, not just now. I–I seem to have forgotten what I wanted to talk to you about, but I'm sure I'll think of it later. When I do, I'll call you." With a wide grin spread across his face, he gave a quick nod to the group and spun on his heels toward the door.

Greg felt as though he were walking on air. As soon as he stepped outside the office and filled his lungs with the fresh autumn air, he began to whistle. The sun was shining, the squirrels were playing, and this was going to be one beautiful day!

❧

Libby returned to the solitude of her private office and closed the door. She had no idea what the conference was about in the front office, but she was sure it bode no good news for her. She buried herself in her work and tried to put Selena Watson out of her mind.

She was not surprised when, thirty minutes later, Michael knocked on her door before opening it. "May I come in?"

"Of course, Michael. Any time. Come in and sit down." Libby tried to keep her tone light and cheerful, but one look at Michael's face told her this visit was going to be anything but sociable.

"I think I'd rather stand." Michael positioned himself directly across from Libby and shuffled his feet. Positioning his briefcase on the floor, he used both hands to lean his weight against her desk. "Libby, you know I'm trying every way I can to help you, but I just can't understand you sometimes. Are you sure you really want this job?" His eyes pierced hers like two sharp arrows.

"What is it, Michael? What have I done wrong? I'm trying to do everything the way you want me to."

"Are you, Libby? Then maybe you can explain this." He bent down to the floor and lifted his briefcase onto her desk. Unlocking the hinges, he reached inside and extracted a folded page of newsprint. "Selena could hardly wait to get to me this morning to show me an article which appeared in yesterday's paper." He unfolded the newspaper and held it up for Libby to see.

Libby gasped and felt the blood drain from her face. In the days following Celia's surgery, she had completely forgotten about the art show, the photographer, and the whole crazy scene that took place at Danny's school over a week ago.

Her hands trembled as she reached for the paper and saw her own face staring back at her. Next to her, Greg was leaning toward her in a possessive stance, and the top of Danny's head was plainly visible in the background. "MR. AND MRS. GREG CUNNINGHAM," the caption read, "PROUD PARENTS OF SECOND-GRADE ARTIST DANNY CUNNINGHAM."

"Is there something you want to tell me?" Michael asked in a voice devoid of emotion. "I seem to be the last to know what's going on around here."

"I—there's nothing to know, Michael. This is not what it seems." Libby was so aghast that she could hardly draw in enough air to talk. "There is a perfectly logical explanation for this. Sit down and let me try to tell you from the beginning exactly what happened."

❧

Greg spent the rest of the morning packing his clothes and office equipment into boxes. Before the weekend was over, he and Danny would be moved into their new home and the condo would be ready for his mother's return from Michigan. But his euphoria lasted all through the morning.

Now that he had identified Michael as Libby's employer rather than her sweetheart, he had a whole new outlook on the situation. The one thing he still could not understand, though, was why Libby's boss should object to her dating someone he didn't even know. What business was it of his, anyway? Michael Phillips must be a tyrant to work for—a real male chauvinist who tried to control his employees with an iron hand.

But Libby had a strong mind of her own. Greg had trouble understanding why she would allow her boss to dictate her personal life. Was it possible she had misunderstood his invitation, thinking he expected her to leave work early to go out and see his house? That must be the reason she felt that Michael would disapprove. Greg could think of no other plausible explanation.

He would talk to Libby again this afternoon and try to explain the whole mix-up. Then perhaps they could start all over again by riding out to see the new house after she finished work. He would try again to tempt her with the new Chinese restaurant that had been getting rave reviews in the newspaper. He would ask Mrs. Caruthers to keep Danny for the evening so he and Libby could have some time together to get better acquainted. He felt excited just thinking about it.

thirteen

Libby's head was bent over a wide spreadsheet, analyzing the list of residents who were delinquent with their maintenance fees. She would try to call each one this afternoon with a gentle reminder, just to keep all of her records up to date.

Following her talk with Michael this morning, she felt it was only a matter of time before she would be turning over all the Blue Dolphin records to someone new. After the write-up in the Sunday paper, she'd be lucky if she were offered any kind of job at all here. The best she could hope for at this point would be a good letter of recommendation.

When Lorraine buzzed to say that she had a visitor, Libby folded the bulky pages and laid them aside. "Who is it, Lorraine?"

"Greg Cunningham," came her secretary's reply. "He would like to speak to you privately." Lorraine's formal tone let Libby know Greg must be standing right beside her, and that any personal conversation between the two of them was out of the question.

"Tell him to come in."

When Greg walked through the doorway, her heart did the funny little skip that his presence always seemed to bring on. What was there about him that robbed her of every smattering of her good sense and judgment? For a long time, she had tried to deny any attraction to this man she knew to be in love with someone else, and who, according to his own son, would soon be getting married. And yet, in spite of all her best efforts to the contrary, Greg Cunningham had the maddening ability to turn her steel willpower into mush.

The minute she stood to greet him, her knees started shaking like two leaves on a windy day. She tried to keep her voice steady. "You must have thought of what it was you wanted to say to me this morning," she said, recalling his strange behavior when he came in earlier to give her his maintenance check.

"Yes. Yes, I did. Can I sit down and talk to you for a few minutes?"

Libby sank back into her chair, grateful for an excuse to take the weight off her wobbly legs. Now that Michael had shown her a copy of Sunday's newspaper, she suspected Greg might have come to apologize. But the damage from that picture had already been done, and it was too late for apologies.

"I wanted to explain about the other day when I asked you to come out and see my new house."

"Oh, yes," Libby said, trying to focus her eyes anywhere other than on Greg's face. "I remember. You, uh. . .hung up rather abruptly before I had a chance to explain why I couldn't go."

"I was wrong to do that, Libby. I'm sorry I was so rude. I guess I just knew how much I wanted you to go with me, and. . ."

"And tomorrow you're moving. That's a big job, isn't it?" Libby groped for a comfortable level of conversation, steering him away from mention of anything personal.

"Not so bad in our case, because Danny and I don't have any furniture to move. Just our clothes and a few other personal belongings. We've known from the get-go that this was a temporary living arrangement, so we haven't unloaded all of our junk in Mom's condo. We have a storage unit across town for most of our stuff."

Greg shifted positions in his chair and leaned forward, trying to establish eye contact with her. "We're already packed, and we'll be out of the condo before Mom gets here next week.

Say, I don't suppose you could go with us to look for furniture this weekend, could you? I'm going to need some new things, and I'm afraid Danny and I are kind of domestically challenged."

"Oh, no, Greg. I really couldn't." Apparently he still did not understand.

"I'm not talking about going during your working hours. I thought maybe Saturday afternoon, we could. . ."

"You never did give me a chance to explain when you called the other day, but the company I work for, Four Star Property Managers, has a strict policy that forbids its employees from fraternizing with the residents of the condominiums in which they work. And to be perfectly honest, I'm in so much trouble with them already—"

"Trouble? What kind of trouble could you possibly be in, Libby?"

Libby heaved a deep sigh and reached inside her desk drawer to pull out the incriminating newspaper. "Have you seen this?" she asked, spreading the page so that Greg could see the picture and its caption. And from the expression on his face, she knew for certain she had caught him totally unaware.

"Oh, my!" He held the paper up for a closer view. "I had no idea. But it's really a very nice picture, if—"

"Nice!" Libby rose to her feet. "Greg Cunningham, do you realize this picture has probably cost me my job here at Blue Dolphin, and all the things I have worked for over these past two years?"

All color drained from Greg's face. "No! Oh, they wouldn't!" Then seeing the desolate expression on her face, he reached across the desk for her hands. "Libby, I am so sorry. Don't you know the very last thing in the world I would ever want to do is to make trouble for you? Libby, I lo—" He stopped short of saying the words on the tip of his tongue, words that came as a surprise even to himself. *Where did those words come from?*

"I—think highly of you," he finished lamely. "I would never knowingly hurt you."

Libby pulled her hands free of his and sank back onto her chair. "It's all right, Greg. It doesn't matter now, anyway. I think this was just one more nail in my coffin."

"Look, Libby. I want to make this up to you. I don't know how I can do that, but I'll think of some way. And please say you'll let me take you out for dinner this weekend. By then, I won't be a Blue Dolphin resident any longer, so you won't be breaking any rule."

And what would Tiffany say about that? As much as Libby longed to accept his invitation, she felt a pang of disappointment that he would be so disloyal to his fiancée. "No, Greg, it—it just wouldn't be right. But thanks for asking me. I know you're just trying to compensate for the damage done by the picture, but really, that was just as much my fault as yours. I had no business going to that art show in the first place."

Greg did not try to disguise the hurt on his face. He looked as though she had given him a resounding slap. "Okay, then. I'll just run along. I doubt I'll be seeing you again, Libby, because Danny and I are clearing out of here tomorrow."

Their eyes met and held as she stood to bid him good-bye. Libby fought back her tears. She wouldn't let herself be humiliated by showing him how much she cared. She started to circle her desk to walk him out when he suddenly exclaimed, *"Stop! Don't take another step!"*

A cold chill enveloped her body. Was there a snake loose in the office, or what was the big emergency? "What? What is it, Greg?"

"My contact lens," he explained. "I brushed a t—a speck of dust out of my eye, and the thing just popped out." He bent and groped around on the carpet. "Don't take a step. You might crush it. Just stand there for a minute while I find it. It has to be right here." He shed his shoes, dropped to his knees, and began raking his fingers through the carpet.

"I'll help." Libby slid out of her pumps, and in her stocking feet, edged her way around the desk on all fours, running her fingers through the soft nylon pile.

"I found it!" Greg exclaimed, at the precise moment when their heads met and collided with a gentle thud. "We've got to quit meeting like this," he quipped, looking up into her shining eyes.

The accelerating sounds of their merriment grew, fueled by emotions held too long in abeyance, carried into the outer office and probably beyond. When the office door opened, both Libby and Greg in their stocking feet faced each other on all fours, with tears of laughter streaming down their cheeks.

"What in the world is going on in here?" Libby recognized Selana Watson's high-pitched voice. Lifting her eyes to the doorway, she looked up into the shocked faces of Michael Phillips, Selena Watson, and Adam Ridgefield.

fourteen

On Monday, the nurse helped Celia pack her few belongings into her overnight case. "We're going to miss you around here."

"And I'm going to miss all this royal treatment," Celia said, but her smile laid bare her overflowing joy to be going home at last. Libby spread out the clothes she had brought for Celia to wear home and helped her put them on.

"Poor Libby. These nurses have me so spoiled that I'm sure I'll be hard for you to manage."

Libby forced a smile. "I'll manage." What should have been a happy day for Libby was clouded by the memory of the embarrassing moments of last Friday, and the dismal realization that Greg and Danny had moved out of her life forever. But of course, she had not shared any of this with Celia. In fact, Celia was still holding fast to the belief that Libby was firmly ensconced as permanent manager of the Blue Dolphin Condominiums, and Libby would not correct that mistake until it was absolutely necessary.

At that moment, an aide came through the door pushing a wheelchair. Celia gave it a scornful look. "I don't need that thing," she declared. "I'm perfectly able to walk out of here."

"Sorry, Miss Malone. Doctor's orders." While the nurse seated Celia in the chair and pushed her into the hall, Libby and the aide stacked Celia's overnight case and her floral arrangements onto a flower cart and followed them down the hall to the elevators.

Libby brought her car up to the door and the nurse helped Celia into the front seat. Then, after a few more good-byes and waves, the sisters were on their way at last.

"I'm so happy to be going home, Libby. But I can see this has all been a big strain on you. The lines of worry are written all over your face. You're looking very tired, and it's no wonder. You've been juggling trips to the hospital, your work at Blue Dolphin, and running the house. I'm going to try not to be a lot of trouble for you once I get home."

"I'm fine. And it's high time I got to be the caretaker in this family, Celia. It's just so great to be taking you back where you belong. God has certainly been good to us."

When they reached their house, Libby supported Celia up the steps, noting her sister was still very weak and frail. "Now, you go right to bed, Celia—doctor's orders. I'll see to getting your things inside, and then I'm going to run to the grocery to get all the makings for a big pot of soup. I'm going to put some meat on those bones of yours if it kills me."

Celia tried to protest going to bed in the middle of the day, but Libby was insistent. She pulled back the clean sheets and fluffed the pillow. "There, now. I'll get you a glass of juice before I go. Is there anything else you'd like before I leave?"

"Just my Bible, please, Libby. I have so much to be thankful for."

"We both do, Honey," Libby agreed. She brought in Celia's bag and unpacked it. Then she arranged the vases of flowers around her room and put her Bible, along with a glass of chilled orange juice, on her bedside table. Leaning over to kiss her sister's forehead, she said again, "We both have much to be thankful for, Celia!" Libby knew she would need to keep reminding herself of that thought through the difficult days ahead.

An hour later, Libby returned from the store, the back seat of her car filled with grocery bags. Pulling into the drive, she was surprised to see a late-model sports car parked beside the curb.

Her arms loaded with groceries, she hurried inside to find out who that unfamiliar car belonged to. "Hello, Celia! I'm home!" She dropped the groceries on the kitchen table and went directly to Celia's bedroom.

When Libby saw Dr. Jennings seated in a chair beside Celia's bed, her heart lurched. Had her sister called the doctor because, in her absence, she had taken a turn for the worse? "What is it, Doctor? Is Celia all right?"

"Why, by the looks of her, I'd say she is getting along just fine," Dr. Jennings said, rising to his feet.

Celia, seeing the look of alarm on Libby's face, hastened to assure her. "Bob—Dr. Jennings—just stopped by on his way home from his office. He wanted to make sure we made it home safely."

The pallor of Celia's face that Libby had noted earlier in the day had now been transformed into a rosy glow, and there was a fresh bouquet of pink rosebuds on the dresser. *Of course! Why didn't I see this earlier?* For the first time that Libby could ever remember, her sister had a beau, and a very distinguished one at that.

Time after time over the years, Libby had heard Celia refuse invitations from would-be suitors because she had to work, had to study, or was just too tired to go out again after a busy day. Libby could not have been happier for her!

"I'll just leave you two to chat, then, while I go to the kitchen and fix supper. If you like soup, Dr. J—um, Bob—there'll be plenty."

"I love soup," the doctor exclaimed with enthusiasm. And Celia continued to glow.

While Libby worked in the kitchen, chopping and peeling and putting together a hearty pot of beef minestrone, she heard the distant sound of sirens. The hospital was several miles away, but occasionally when several emergency vehicles blasted their signals at the same time, the sound carried through the trees.

Libby's flesh crawled with an uneasy feeling, but she brushed it aside. Her sister was safe at home now, and except for the uncertainty of her future employment, everything was going to be just fine.

When supper was ready, Libby helped Celia into her pretty quilted robe, and Bob escorted her into the dining room. Seated around the table, the three of them laughed and talked as they enjoyed bowl after bowl of soup and crusty loaves of hot garlic bread. Libby was delighted to see that Celia's appetite was almost as healthy as her own.

Still, Libby's strange feelings of apprehension remained throughout supper, so when the telephone rang, she jumped up from her chair and ran to answer it. "Hello?"

"Libby, it's Lorraine. Did you catch the six o'clock news on the local television station?"

"No, Lorraine. What happened?"

"There's been a terrible automobile accident out on Highway 98. A car collided with a semi. The pictures on the news looked just awful. I don't see how anyone could have survived that crash."

"Oh, how terrible!" Libby said. "Were there local people involved?"

"That's why I called you, Libby. They've just released the names of the drivers of the two vehicles, and one of them was Lenore Cunningham."

"Oh, no! Is she—" Libby left the half-finished sentence dangling in midair.

"Thank God, she's still alive. They've taken both victims to the hospital. They think the driver of the semi is going to be all right, but Lenore is listed in critical condition. I'm sorry to be the bearer of such bad news, but I was sure you'd want to know about it."

"Yes. Thanks for thinking of me, Lorraine. Call me if you hear anything further." Libby let the receiver drop back onto its base. She stood frozen to the spot, paralyzed, her head reeling from the shock. Greg must be devastated. What could she do to help?

જ

Bob Jennings drove Libby to the hospital. She had offered no protest when he told her she was in no condition to drive.

His sleek little sports car slid through the traffic and pulled up in the physicians' parking lot within a matter of minutes. "You won't be able to go into the emergency room with me, Libby, but there's a waiting area where you can sit down and have a cup of coffee while you wait. I'll be able to go in and find out just what Mrs. Cunningham's injuries are and what kind of condition she's in, and I promise to come out and report to you just as soon as I know anything."

Libby gave him a grateful smile and watched him go through the big double doors marked EMERGENCY ROOM. AUTHORIZED PERSONNEL ONLY.

The only thing left for her to do now was to pray. *Dear God, please send Your angels to watch over Mrs. Cunningham and keep her safe. And if it's within Your will, please spare her life for Greg's sake, and for Danny.* Following Bob Jennings's suggestion, she headed for the emergency waiting room.

It was so crowded that she did not see him at first. Then she spotted Greg seated on the edge of a chair, his head buried in his hands. *He must be praying.* When he looked up and saw her, he stood and they met halfway across the room.

As though it were the most natural thing in the world, Libby fell into his arms and let his tears fall into her hair. "Oh, Greg, I'm so sorry. Have you heard anything yet?"

"No, Libby. Only that it's very bad. They won't let me be in there with her. As soon as they stabilize her, they're going to take her upstairs to surgery. . .if she makes it that long." His voice cracked and Libby ran her hands over his shoulders to offer whatever comfort she could.

"I prayed you'd come, Libby, and somehow I just knew you would."

"I came as soon as I heard. Where's Danny?"

"He's staying at a friend's house. He wanted to come, but I didn't think he should until we know more about Mom's condition."

"Is there anyone you want me to call?"

"I've already called my sister in Virginia. Patty will get a flight and be here just as soon as she can. Neither of us can really believe what has happened."

Libby led him to a couch. "Let's sit here," she suggested. "Would you like for me to get you a cup of coffee?"

"I couldn't swallow a thing right now, Libby. It's just very comforting to have you here with me while I wait."

Libby wondered why Tiffany was not there beside the man who would soon be her husband. Perhaps she was out of town, for surely she would be there to offer her comfort and support if she knew. Libby started to ask Greg if he wanted her to call Tiffany, but she didn't think she should. Instead, the two of them sat in silence, holding hands and waiting for the emergency room doors to open.

fifteen

The waiting room was filled with people, all of whom wore the same weary expressions of pain and apprehension. And each time the desk phone rang or the double doors swung open, every one of them looked up with a mixture of hope and guarded anxiety. Libby's heart ached for all of them, but most of all for the man seated beside her.

At last, Bob Jennings came through the door. He had changed into hospital scrubs, and a surgical mask hung from his neck. He walked directly to where Libby and Greg were seated, and they stood to meet him.

"It's not good," he told them. He drew the two of them into a corner where they could speak with a modicum of privacy. "You must be the son Libby has told me about. Greg, I'm sorry to be the bearer of such grim news. I'm sure your mother's doctors will come out and talk to you in a few minutes. They're doing everything they possibly can, but—"

"When can I see her?"

"I expect they'll come out to get you very soon now. They'll want you to see her for a few minutes, and then they'll ask you to help them make some very hard decisions."

Greg shook his head as though trying to loosen the cobwebs. "I don't understand. I'm not qualified to make their decisions. I just want them to save my mother's life, and whatever it takes, that's what they must do."

"Here they come now," Bob said, pointing to the two doctors who had just come through the ER doors, and Greg rushed forward to meet them.

"Let's step into the hall," one of the doctors suggested. "We need to talk."

"How is my mother? Is she still holding her own? Is there any sign of improvement?"

Libby tried to stay behind in the waiting room as the doctors led Greg into the adjoining hallway, but he reached for her hand, and she had no choice but to follow.

The doctors exchanged looks, one of them gave a slight nod, and the other one spoke. "Mr. Cunningham, I'm Dr. Chang and this is Dr. Bollinger. We regret to tell you that your mother is slipping away from us. She is losing blood faster than we can put it back into her body. She appears to have internal hemorrhaging that we aren't able to locate without surgery, and in her extremely weakened condition, we do not believe she could survive such extensive surgery."

"What are you saying?" Greg said, shaking his head in disbelief. "What then is the alternative?"

Again the doctors exchanged glances, and Libby could tell that this conversation was not easy for them either.

"Actually, there are only two," Dr. Bollinger replied. "In a moment, we're going to take you in to see her, but you must prepare yourself for a shock. What we do after that will depend on your decision. We can send her upstairs to a team of specialists who can perform exploratory surgery and put her through what will probably be hours of useless stress, or we can make her as comfortable as possible and let nature take its course. In our opinion, the end result is going to be the same, but the decision is yours to make."

"Let me see her," Greg whispered. He was still gripping Libby's hand when the doctors led them toward the emergency room, and although both doctors gave her a questioning look, they did not protest when Greg kept her by his side.

Lenore Cunningham lay pale and lifeless on a gurney, a maze of tubes attached to her motionless body. Her face was lacerated, bruised, and swollen beyond recognition. A heartbeat recording steady beeps on a monitor provided the only visible sign that this woman was still alive. Greg stepped forward, and with tears running down his cheeks, he brushed a light kiss on her forehead. He whispered words into her ear that Libby could not hear, and of course, his mother did not show any response at all.

Standing over her limp body, Greg closed his eyes and paused for a moment, and Libby sensed that he was praying. She lifted her own silent prayer for the woman whose life seemed to be slipping away before their eyes.

"We'd better move on now, Mr. Cunningham," one of the doctors urged gently. "You must help us make our decision, and we don't have time to waste. Can you tell us what you want us to do?"

"Yes, Doctor." Greg spoke without hesitation. "I want you to go ahead with the surgery. To you, this operation may seem hopeless, but I know that with God, all things are possible." He squeezed Libby's hand, and she returned the gesture, trying to send him a sign of her faith.

"We know that, Mr. Cunningham. We have seen seemingly impossible things happen right here in this hospital, and we'll be praying for a miracle. But I must warn you to prepare yourself for the worst. If there is anyone else you need to call. . ."

"I've called my sister in Virginia. She's already on her way. I've called my pastor, too. He has a wedding scheduled for this evening, but he's getting a prayer chain started. He'll be here later this evening."

The second doctor handed Greg a pen and two sheets of printed material. "We'll have to ask you to sign these consent papers, Mr. Cunningham. We both pray your decision will turn out to be a wise one."

Greg's hand shook so that his signature looped crazily across the page. "It's the only decision I can make under the circumstances. I'll be praying God will bless and guide the hands of the doctors who'll be performing the surgery."

"We'll be moving her up to the fifth floor for the surgery,"

Dr. Chang said. "There's a lounge at the end of the hall where you can wait until we have further news."

As though walking through a bad dream, Greg led Libby out of the emergency room and silently they started down the hall toward the elevators.

Libby had forgotten all about Bob Jennings. He caught up with them at the elevator doors. "I'm going to run out to your house and check on Celia," he told her. "I know she's worrying about what's going on. Do you want to come along now? There's really nothing more you can do here."

"No, Bob. I appreciate all of your help, but I think Greg needs a friend by his side right now even more than Celia needs me. I don't want to leave him here all alone, and I know my sister would want me to stay for as long as I'm needed."

"I understand. Do you want to call me when you're ready to go home, or shall I come back in an hour or so to check on you?"

"It's not necessary," she said. "I can get a taxi." She felt she had troubled him enough for one night. She was just so grateful he would be there to check on Celia. It was as though he had been sent by God to help them all through their troubles. He had been their family doctor for several years, yet only recently had she thought of him as a personal friend.

"Don't even think of calling a taxi, Libby. Just take my card and promise you'll call me when you're ready to go." He handed her a card from his wallet, and noting her hesitation, he added, "It will relieve Celia's mind, and I'm sure she'll be able to rest easier if she knows you'll call me whenever you're ready to go home."

Put like that, how could she refuse? Libby had an impulse to reach up and kiss him on the cheek, but that would be much too familiar. Instead, she offered him her hand. "Thanks for everything, Bob. I don't know how we would have gotten through this without you."

"You're not through it yet, Libby, but be strong for Greg.

He's going to need all the help he can get, tonight and in the days ahead."

&

The first light of a new day slanted through the double glass windows of the fifth-floor lounge. Libby uncurled from the cold leather couch where she had caught intermittent moments of sleep throughout the long night. Greg had tossed and turned in the recliner beneath the window, but at last he seemed to be sleeping peacefully, his long legs hanging over the end of the chair. A kind nurse had brought them both pillows and blankets, and told them where to find fresh coffee from the nurses' station whenever they wanted it.

Libby looked at her watch. Five-thirty, and still no word from the doctors! When she stood and stretched, every muscle in her body protested.

She walked down the hall to the nurses' station and poured herself a cup of steaming coffee.

"Cream and sugar?" a young woman in a white uniform asked her.

"No thanks. Just black." Libby smiled her gratitude and walked back to the lounge. She remained standing, looking out the windows, while she sipped her coffee.

She watched the sparse flow of traffic on the street below. She thought of Danny staying with his friend, while at a nearby hospital life ebbed from his beloved grandmother's body.

At first she was not aware that Greg was awake and watching her, but when she saw his open eyes, she said, "I'll go down and get you some coffee. What should I put in it?"

"Just black," he said. He looked at his watch. "Do you suppose those doctors forgot about us? Maybe we're in the wrong place. Shouldn't we know something by now?"

Although those same thoughts had crossed Libby's mind, she tried to sound reassuring when she said, "No, this is where they told us to come. They'll let us know something as soon as they can. Maybe no news is good news. It must mean your mother is still in there fighting for her life."

She left and came back with his coffee and handed it to him. When he reached to take it from her, Libby noticed his hands shook so badly that he spilled a few drops on her wrist. "Oh, sorry," he mumbled.

They sat together on the couch, drinking their coffee and saying few words.

"It was nice of your minister to come by last night and spend so much time with you," Libby said.

"Reverend Hall is a good man. His visit helped me a lot." He looked at his watch again. "I'll be glad when Patty can get here. We need to be facing this thing together."

Again Greg lapsed into silence, tilting the last drops of coffee from his Styrofoam cup. Then, pitching his cup into the trash can, he slipped an arm around Libby's shoulder and said, "Libby, I wish there were some words I could say— some way I could let you know—just what your presence here has meant to me." Libby could feel heat rising to her cheeks, but she was quiet as he continued. "You don't have to stay here with me any longer. I know you have obligations you need to be taking care of, and I'll be okay for now. Reverend Hall said he would come back again today. His visit last night was a real blessing to me."

When Libby made no move to leave, he repeated, "Go on home now, Libby, and take care of yourself. I'll be all right."

Libby considered his words. She had found herself drowning in the intimacy of these last few hours they had spent together. Ever since Danny had told her of Greg's impending marriage, she had tried to steel herself against the growing love she felt for him, but his need of her last night had overshadowed all her earlier resolve.

Even realizing that to Greg her actions had been a simple outpouring of friendship, for her they had meant so much more. And although she knew she was only increasing the heartache she would suffer in the end, there was no way she could turn her back on him now.

While she sat pondering her dilemma, approaching foot-steps in the hall caught their attention. They jumped to their feet to meet the doctors.

"Is she—?" Greg could not finish his question. His face was lined and haggard, and Libby imagined she could almost hear the hammering of his heart.

"We've found the source of her hemorrhaging," the surgeon reported. "Your mother had a ruptured spleen which we had to remove. We also had to remove one badly damaged kidney. There were also—"

"But how *is* she?" Greg insisted. The details would come later, but for now, the most important part was the condition of his mother.

"Mr. Cunningham, I wish we could say your mother is out of the woods, and that we could give you a promise she is going to be fine, but we still have a long way to go. About all we can tell you at this point is that her heart seems to be strong, and she is holding her own. After we get her stabilized from her surgery, we'll be cleaning her up and moving her into intensive care. There you'll be allowed to visit her for a few minutes every two hours, but don't expect her to respond to you, or even to recognize you.

"They won't have her ready to transfer for another hour yet, so you have time to get a bite of breakfast in the cafeteria downstairs. We'll be talking to you, giving you updated reports off and on during the day, but for now, we need to get a little rest ourselves. It's been a long night. I would advise that, as soon as you have seen your mother, you try to do the same. There is nothing more you can do for her here."

Greg tried to thank them, but they were already hurrying down the hall. Libby wondered how they could continue to work with steady hands for such long, tense hours without a break.

"Greg, you'll want to stay around long enough to see your

mother, but I think I'll call Bob to come pick me up now. I need to go home and have a shower before I go to work this morning."

"Oh, Libby. It was so selfish of me to keep you here all night. Can you forgive me? I just didn't stop to think that you'd have to go to work this morning."

"This was where I wanted to be. I'm just glad I could be here when you needed someone." Again Libby wondered about Tiffany. Why wasn't she here beside the man she loved, helping him through these torturous hours? "Will you call and let me know if there's a change?" she asked. "I know you have a lot of things pressing on your mind, but everyone at Blue Dolphin will be calling me to find out."

"I'll call you," he promised. He pulled her close to him and said in a voice that trembled with emotion, "I'll call you no matter what."

"Is there anything I can do for you before I leave?"

He lowered his eyes and hesitated. "Well, yes, there is one thing. But you've done so much, I hate to ask for more."

"Just ask. Whatever it is, I'll be happy to do it if I can."

"Well, there's a little prayer chapel on the first floor. Would you go downstairs and pray with me for a few minutes before you leave?"

Libby was moved to tears. "Of course I will, Greg. I've been praying for your mother all through the night, and I know you have too, but praying in the chapel together will be very special. Let's go."

The little room was dark except for two glowing candles, their steady flames reflecting on the large brass cross in the center of the altar. Recorded organ music played softly in the background. *A mighty fortress is our God. . .*

Kneeling side by side before the tiny altar, Libby and Greg lifted their prayers to Almighty God, while upstairs in a narrow bed, Lenore Cunningham continued to fight her battle, holding onto the fragile thread of life.

sixteen

By the time Libby arrived at her desk on Tuesday morning, she was too stressed to admit or even realize that she was tired beyond thinking clearly. She moved through the morning like a robot, automatically performing the tasks of her daily routine.

She had given Lorraine a full report on Lenore Cunningham's condition, at least to the extent that she knew it, and asked her secretary to field all calls so that she would not have to rehash those painful moments with each person who asked. "Unless Greg calls," she added. "Of course I'd want you to put through any calls from him."

The phone rang incessantly. Libby could hear Lorraine repeat the same phrases over and over again. In between calls, the thoughtful secretary kept the ceramic mug on Libby's desk filled with fresh, hot coffee.

In spite of the uninterrupted solitude that Lorraine carefully orchestrated for her, Libby still had a hard time concentrating on her work. Her immediate concern was for Greg and his mother, and of course for Danny too. But there were other matters weighing heavily on her mind. As soon as she could leave Blue Dolphin for the day, she'd run home to check on Celia. If Greg had not called her with a report by then, she'd swing over to the hospital and see what she could find out about Lenore.

As if these worries were not enough, there still loomed the threat of Selena and Adam, and the almost certainty that her days here at Blue Dolphin were numbered. After the fiasco last Friday afternoon when Greg lost his contact lens and the two of them were caught scrambling around on the floor like a couple of crazy schoolkids, she was lucky to even be allowed back in here today.

And as soon as she managed to push those worries aside, her thoughts turned back to Celia. She thanked God a thousand times a day for her sister's progress. Her heavenly Father had heard their prayers and was answering them in a wonderful way.

She wondered if God thought she was ungrateful or lacked sufficient faith because she continued to worry about those mounting hospital and doctor bills. She had urged Celia not to worry about them, and she had meant that with all her heart. Celia's health was priceless, and yet the bills were a reality that would have to be faced sooner or later.

But suppose there was no money coming in to pay them? The thought of joining the ranks of the unemployed was a possibility too frightening to even think about. Libby now had a mile-long list of things she was trying *not* to think about, and that fact alone was mind-boggling.

It was no use. Libby decided she might as well clear off her desk and leave for the morning. She was useless here at Blue Dolphin today. If her absence triggered Selena's anger again, then she would just have to deal with that later.

"Lorraine, I'm going home. I'm sorry, but I can't even think straight until I catch a few z's. If anyone needs me, just tell them I'll try to get back out here this afternoon and respond to my messages."

"Go ahead, Libby. I really think the people here—even the most unreasonable of the bunch—understand where your priorities need to be right now. We've had dozens of people calling to help Mrs. Cunningham. Quite a few of them have offered to donate blood. I've referred all of those to the hospital blood bank. Then there have been offers to keep Danny, or to send food, run errands, or do whatever would be of help." She handed Libby a sheet of paper torn from a yellow legal pad, with a long, handwritten list of names and telephone numbers. Beside each name was an offer of some specific kind of help. "If you see Greg, would you pass these along to him?"

Libby studied the paper. "This is amazing. Look, here's Mr. Kalinski offering to keep an eye on Danny. He's the man who complained about Danny's practicing his casting in the backyard. And Mrs. Caruthers is organizing a community-wide prayer chain. She's offering to keep Danny after school and have him stay at her condo all night. Danny always likes going to her condo. This list goes on and on, Lorraine. I know Greg will be touched to see he has so many friends here at Blue Dolphin. Sometimes he felt like this whole community was against him."

"You know what they say about 'when the going gets tough.' " Lorraine said. "That's when the tough get going. And speaking of going, you'd better get out of here before someone comes in needing you for something else."

"I'm gone," Libby called over her shoulder as she headed for the door.

☙

When Libby walked in, she found Celia sitting in the living room watching television from their big recliner, a crocheted granny afghan spread across her knees. Today's newspaper was on the table beside her, folded to show she had completed the daily crossword puzzle and the cryptogram.

"Honestly, Libby, I'm going stark raving mad. I don't mean to complain, but I just can't keep this up much longer. All this inactivity is getting on my nerves. Bob wants me to elevate my leg that had the blood clot, but I think it must surely be dissolved by now. I'm going to ask him when I can get up and start doing things."

Libby chuckled. "What kind of things do you have in mind? Skating? Horseback riding? Waiting tables at the café? Why don't you take advantage of your situation and enjoy being lazy for a change."

"Look who's talking. You're the one who needs to rest today. Did you sleep at all last night?"

"Some," Libby said. "But that's why I'm home early. I'm going to take a shower, catch a quick nap, and then I'm going over to the hospital to see how Mrs. Cunningham is before I go back to work. If the phone rings, don't wake me unless it's important. But if Greg calls—"

"I'll be sure to get you up," Celia finished. She heaved a deep sigh and returned to her television program. "I'm learning how to make a hooked rug," she said. "That Martha Stewart is really something. She can do just about anything. I'll bet *she* never sits down in a recliner to relax."

Libby felt there were so many things she needed to do, and so many places she wanted to be today. She certainly did not have time to relax. But as soon as she stretched out on her bed and snuggled her head on her soft, familiar pillow, she faded into blissful unconsciousness and did not flex a muscle for a solid two hours.

At noon when she awoke from her nap, she felt like a new person, revitalized and as rested as though she had slept for a normal seven hours. And for the first time since yesterday, she suddenly realized she was ravenously hungry.

She heated bowls of leftover minestrone soup from the refrigerator and opened a box of crackers. Cottage cheese and canned peaches substituted for a salad. "Ready for lunch?" she asked Celia, who had come into the kitchen to join her at the table.

"Mmm, that smells so good," Celia declared, spreading a paper napkin over her lap. "We ate so much of your minestrone last night, I'm surprised there was enough for lunch today. Bob certainly seemed to enjoy it, didn't he?"

"Yes, he—" But before Libby could finish her reply, the phone rang and she ran to answer it. Maybe it would be Greg. She hoped it would not be Lorraine calling to tell her that Selena and Michael were looking for her. "Hello?"

"Hey, Libby. I called your office and Lorraine told me you had gone home for a break. I hated to bother you when I know how much you need rest, but I have a small problem, and I wasn't sure who else I should call."

Greg's voice on the line filled Libby with guarded emotion. Was he calling with good news or bad? "I'm glad you called me, Greg. I asked you to. How is your mother?"

In a voice garbled from worry and lack of sleep, he said, "She's holding on, but the doctors still aren't giving me a lot of hope. The thing is, my sister Patty just called. She just landed at the Palm Beach International Airport. That's thirty miles from here, and she can't seem to locate a rental car. They told her it'll be at least two hours before one is available, and even then, it's not a certainty. I really hate to put this burden on you, Libby, but I just can't leave the hospital until I know Mom's going to be all right. Do you know of someone I could hire to drive down and pick her up? I don't mind paying whatever they ask. I just can't get out to make the necessary arrangements right now."

"Oh, Greg, of course. I know lots of people who'd be willing to go for you. In fact, I have a whole list of people who are trying to find some way to help. But I'd like to pick up your sister myself. That is, unless you'd rather have someone else do it. I could leave right now, and save the time it would take to make other arrangements."

"I can't ask you to do that."

She cut his protest short. "Consider it done. I guess you'll be talking to your sister again to let her know what you've worked out. Tell her to meet me in the lower level by the luggage pickup area." Libby glanced across the room at Celia's flowers. "Let her know I'll be carrying a red carnation in my hand."

"She came in on Delta 1289. Right now she's at gate 148 in concourse B. I'll let her know where to look for you. But Libby—"

"Let's don't waste any more time arguing about this, Greg.

Just get word to Patty to pick up her luggage and wait for me there, and I'm outta here."

≈

Forty minutes later, Libby followed the curving drive into Palm Beach International Airport. Following the posted directions, she drove her car to the lower level and hoped Patty would be looking for her. Double-parking by the automatic doors, she clutched a rather wilted long-stemmed red carnation in her hand and hurried to the sidewalk.

"Hold it! You can't leave your car there, young lady."

Libby was just about to explain to the officer when a petite brunette in a yellow suit ran toward her. "You must be Libby Malone," she said. When Libby nodded, she rattled on, "Greg told me you were coming, but I didn't expect you to get here so fast. My, you must have flown. Have you heard any more news of my mother?" Libby detected near hysteria in the distraught woman's rapid fire of words.

"No, Patty, I'm sorry." Libby gave her a quick hug and helped her load her two leather suitcases into the car trunk, under the stern observation of the police officer. "If you've talked to Greg since I left home, then you have a more recent report than I do. Come on; we have to move out of here."

Patty put her carry-on in the back seat of the Avalon, slid into the front beside Libby, and the two of them were on their way.

"Traffic is horrendous at this time of the day," Libby told her, "and you don't get a view of the beaches from here; just lots of tall buildings." Libby continued trying to make pleasant conversation, but Patty was so filled with anxiety that she was scarcely able to respond to any of it. Libby knew her thoughts were on her mother, and she wished she could help with some words of encouragement. She certainly didn't want to upset Patty even more by revealing the dismal report she and Greg had been given by the doctors.

Finally, Libby gave up the effort of talking and flipped the radio to a Christian station. The soothing sounds of gospel music harmonized by an all-male quartet surrounded them as they wove in and out of Palm Beach traffic to the interstate, and then north toward Stuart and the Martin Memorial Hospital where Greg was waiting for them.

When they arrived at the hospital, Libby pulled her car under the canopy of the main entrance. "I'm going to let you off here by the front door, Patty. I'll have to find a place to park, and that may take a little time. But the ladies in pink will direct you to the ICU waiting room where Greg will be expecting you. Just tell them you're Lenore Cunningham's daughter, and they'll take care of you."

"Libby, I don't know how to thank you. Greg told me—"

"Please, Patty. Not now. We can talk about that later. And don't worry about your suitcases. I suppose you'll be staying at either Greg's new house or at your mother's condo in Blue Dolphin. I can take you wherever you need to go when you're ready. I'll be inside just as soon as I find a place to park, and we can work out the details then."

Libby circled the hospital parking lot until she found a space to park her car and rode the elevator up to the fifth floor to the waiting room of the intensive care unit. Greg saw her coming and hurried to meet her.

"Libby!" He embraced her so tightly she could hardly breathe. Although she realized his gesture was one of mere gratitude and friendship, it filled her with pleasure nonetheless. She responded by giving his shoulders a comforting caress.

"Patty's in with Mom now," he told her. Only one of us can go in at a time, and only for five minutes every two hours. Of course, I wanted Patty to have that chance. I know seeing Mom like this is going to be a great shock for Patty. Mom's hooked up to all kinds of machines, with tubes going in every direction, and she looks so pale and lifeless."

"Has she regained consciousness?"

"Yes, I think she did for a few minutes. She opened her

eyes and looked at me. I'm sure she recognized me, but she couldn't speak because she has a respirator tube inserted in her throat. It looks terribly uncomfortable, but at least I know she's still alive. I feel like every hour that passes gives us that much more hope."

"You'll never believe how many people have called to offer help, Greg. Look, I have a list of them, and calls were still coming in when I left." She pulled from her purse the list Lorraine had compiled and held it up for Greg to see. "All of these people really want to help, so you mustn't hesitate to call on any of them."

"I see blood donors listed," Greg observed, his eyes traveling down the page. "I'm glad to have this, because the hospital would like for us to replace the units of blood they're giving Mom. Of course, Patty and I will contribute as often as we can, and replacement credit is given for any type of blood donated in Mom's name. There is one problem, though. Mom has O-negative, and the local blood bank is running low on their supply of it. Unfortunately, that's not the most common type. We need to find some donors with O-negative, but both my sister and I have O-positive."

"Yes, that's what I have too," Libby said. "But I'll put out an appeal on the condo bulletin board and maybe we will find some O-negative donors. I'll be going out there before long, and I'll put out the word." Turning her head to look beyond his shoulder, Libby said, "Look, Greg, here comes your sister now."

Patty dabbed at her eyes with a tissue and blew her nose. "Oh, Greg, it's just too awful—"

Greg enfolded his sister in his arms and let her cry on his shoulder. "We just have to put her in God's hands, Patty, and be strong for her, the way she would want us to be. All we can do now is pray."

Libby walked away to let them have their conversation in private. She would leave them soon and return to her office, but first she needed to find out what Patty wanted done with her luggage.

After a few tearful minutes together, brother and sister joined Libby on the leather couch. "We've been talking about our plans," Greg said. "We won't be able to see Mom again for two hours, but we feel one of us needs to stay here in case there is a report of any change. I have my car outside in the parking lot, and Patty is welcome to use it. As soon as she gets back, though, I need to go out and check on Danny. Poor little guy. He's staying with his best friend, but I guess he thinks I've forgotten him."

"Does he know about the accident?" Patty asked.

"He knows his grandma was involved in a wreck and that she's in the hospital, but he doesn't realize how serious it is. I expect he thinks we'll all be coming home together anytime now. I need to see him tonight, to talk with him and try to explain how things are going to be for a while."

Lord, show me how I can help them, Libby prayed. Watching their pain tore at her heartstrings. "What else can I do to help?"

When Libby noted Patty's hesitation, she realized the distraught young woman was reluctant to ask for another favor, but Libby hastened to assure her. "Patty, I really want to help. Please tell me what you need."

Patty's grateful smile told Libby her guess had been correct, even before Patty confessed. "Greg gave me directions to Mom's condo, but I've never driven in this city before, and I'm really afraid I might get lost," she said. "Greg thought he heard you say you were going back out to Blue Dolphin this afternoon, so if you'd let me follow you, I could put my things in Mom's condo. I need to freshen up from the trip and change out of this wool suit into something more suitable for Florida weather. I could do all that and still get back here to the hospital before our next visitation period."

"I have a better idea," Libby suggested, brightening at

another opportunity to be useful. "Since your things are already in my car, and since I'm going back to the office for only a short time, I can take you out to Blue Dolphin and make sure you get into the right condo. It's almost time for the condo office to close anyway, so I'll just check my messages while you do whatever you need to do. Then I'll come back to the condo to pick you up. I'll have you back here in plenty of time for your next visitation."

"Libby, that's an imposition. . . ," Greg started to protest, but Patty cut him short.

"I'd feel so much more comfortable with that kind of arrangement, if you're sure you don't mind, Libby. I feel a little shaky right now anyway, and to drive a strange car in a strange city, well, I'd love to accept your offer."

"Then it's all settled," Libby said. "Stay here with your brother a little longer. I'll get my car and pick you up under the canopy of the front entrance in a few minutes." Libby hurried down the hall before they could offer further protests or change their minds. She welcomed another chance to offer them a small bit of comfort, and it surely did help to dispel the ominous black cloud that had hovered over her head all morning long.

seventeen

With Patty in the car beside her, Libby did not stop as they passed the Blue Dolphin administration building. "That's where I work," she pointed out, but continued on down Blue Dolphin Drive. There would be time later to come back and check her messages. Right now, she simply wanted to get Patty settled into her mother's condo where she could have some time alone to freshen up and unwind a little.

Libby pulled into the paved area of building 300 and parked. "This is it," she announced, swinging open the car door. Libby opened the trunk and grabbed the largest of the suitcases and Patty followed with the other two. Libby led the way through the courtyard and up the stairs to Lenore's corner apartment. "Do you have the key?"

"Yes, I do," Patty said, setting her valise beside the front door. "Greg gave it to me. It's right here somewhere inside my purse."

Libby noticed that Patty's hands were trembling as she rummaged through the contents of her purse looking for the key. This had to be a very hard time for her. "Would you like for me to come inside with you for just a minute while you catch your breath?"

"Would you, please?" Patty's gratitude spilled from her eyes. She opened the door, and Libby followed her into the foyer.

"I'll help you carry your things back to the bedroom, and then if you're okay, I'll leave you alone to shower and change clothes."

Patty led the way down the hall with Libby right behind her. They set the suitcases on the king-size bed so they could be unpacked with ease.

This is the bed where Greg has slept, Libby mused, allowing her eyes to skim over the tufted coverlet. A quickening of her heart caused her to look away, to focus on the other furniture in the room. "Look, Patty, the message light on the telephone is blinking. Do you think Greg might be trying to reach us?"

Patty gasped. She flew to the phone and punched the button. But it was not Greg's male voice that greeted them. Instead, a sensuous murmur purred softly from the box. "Hi, Greg. It's Tiffany."

Libby wanted to run from the room to avoid hearing any more of the message meant for Greg's ears alone, but Patty stood between her and the doorway, frantically scribbling Tiffany's words on a notepad. Libby turned away and examined her hair in the mirror, trying to project an air of disinterest as Patty allowed the kittenish tones to continue. "Darling, please call me. I tried calling you at your new place, but apparently you don't have your answering machine hooked up yet. I'll be right here waiting for your call."

After a short beep, the same voice came on again, but before the second message progressed beyond the intimate salutation, Libby interrupted. "I'm sorry, Patty. I really do have to get over to my office. I'll come back for you in an hour." She pushed past Patty, who was still jotting down messages from the phone onto her notepad.

"Fine, Libby. Wait a minute; just let me—"

But Libby didn't even slow down. She made a beeline for the balcony and a breath of fresh air, letting the front door slam behind her.

Libby stumbled down the steps, unable to reconcile the emotions Tiffany's messages had stirred within her. Certainly hearing those words of endearment spoken to Greg should not have been a shock to her, because Danny had already told her of his father's impending marriage. But there was something about actually hearing her voice on the line that shifted Tiffany's image from an imaginary figure to one of stark reality.

Libby still could not figure out why Tiffany wasn't the first person Greg had called on the night of the accident. If she was the woman he loved and planned to marry, shouldn't she be the one here beside him instead of Libby, a casual friend? But perhaps Greg *had* tried to call Tiffany that night and had been unable to reach her. Libby was grateful to Lorraine for calling to tell her the terrible news, giving her the opportunity to come to his side and offer whatever comfort she could.

The first thing Greg had done before rushing to his mother's side that night was to make arrangements for Danny's immediate care, Libby surmised. Then he had probably tried to call Tiffany, who happened to be away from her phone. Later, by the time he learned the seriousness of his mother's injuries, Greg had been thrown into such a state of shock that he had not given another thought to making telephone calls. Yes, that must be the way it happened. It seemed like the only logical explanation for the sequence of events that followed.

The messages on his mother's answering machine could have been left there for him days earlier. By now, Greg must surely have talked with Tiffany and explained the situation. Why, in all probability, she was with him at this very moment.

Soon Libby would drive Patty back to the hospital where Patty and Greg would share their anxiety and try to comfort each other. And Tiffany would be there with them to lend them her strength and encouragement. They wouldn't be needing Libby's help again.

That thought should have pleased Libby. She wanted the best for them, didn't she? And who was she to judge whether or not Tiffany was the best one to provide them with the comfort and strength they needed? One shouldn't judge a person just by the tone of her voice.

Libby zoomed out of the parking lot before she remembered the conservative speed limit within the condo complex.

Embarrassed by her own carelessness, she braked to a sedate fifteen miles per hour and claimed her space outside her office.

Because it was after four o'clock, the administration building was locked and deserted. She used her key to enter and found several messages Lorraine had placed on her desk. At least five calls needed to be returned today, but would she have enough time to complete them before taking Patty back to the hospital?

She wanted to get the notice posted on the bulletin board asking for type O-negative blood for Mrs. Cunningham. That was her priority right now. There was no one here to help her—she would have to print and post the notice herself.

She had promised to have Patty back at the hospital for the next visitation period, and that was only an hour away. Late afternoon traffic would be heavy with people on their way home from work or shopping, and Libby certainly didn't want to risk causing Patty to be late.

She flipped on her computer and began to type up the announcement requesting type O-negative blood. She used big, bold lettering that was sure to attract attention. She would put the notice up at once and pray it would bring quick results. Then she could take Patty back to the hospital, even if it meant she would have to return to her office later to finish her work for the day.

ə.

When Greg heard the elevator grind to a halt and the doors slide open, he raised his head from his hands. Seeing his sister step out, he rose and went to meet her.

Patty looked refreshed in a cotton shirtwaist with short sleeves, but anxiety etched her face. "Has there been any change?" she asked.

Greg shook his head. "I haven't seen any of the doctors since you left. The nurses are all so busy, and I don't like to trouble them by asking for information I'm sure they don't have."

Patty looked at her watch. "It will soon be time to go in to see Mom. Maybe we can find out more when they let us see her again."

Greg kept looking toward the elevators. "Isn't Libby coming upstairs?"

"No, she dropped me off by the front door. She said she had some things she needed to tend to. She's awfully nice, isn't she, Greg? Do you have a special interest in her?"

"She's very nice," Greg agreed noncommittally. "I thought she would at least come up to see how things are going." Greg did not attempt to hide the disappointment he felt. "Did she send me any message?"

"No, I don't remember her saying anything like that. Oh, but by the way, you did have some messages on Mom's answering machine. Somebody named Tiffany wants you to call her. She called several times." Patty gave him a questioning look.

"Yes, I suppose I should give Tiffany a call," Greg said with an air of resignation. "I owe her that much. But I've had more important things on my mind lately. I'll try to call her later. But right now, I need to touch base with Danny."

"Have you talked to him today?"

"No, but I tried. I called Mrs. Burbank, the friend who's keeping him. She said the boys had some kind of after-school practice for a school program they're working on. She said her husband would be picking them up after he got off work. Now that you're here, I thought I might use the two-hour interval between visits to take him over to the new house with me while I clean up and shave. It would give us a chance to visit, and we might even grab a bite to eat before I get back. He probably feels neglected."

"Yes, do that," his sister urged. "Things like this are hard on children. Sometimes we adults don't realize how much of our anxiety they pick up and carry with them. A little visit will be good for you both, and I'll be here in case there is any news on Mom."

Greg put an arm around her shoulder and gave her a squeeze. "I'm so glad you're here. Is Stanley managing all right being left at home to fend for himself and the kids?"

"He's fine." Patty smiled. "He's such a great person. I hope someday you'll be able to find someone who can mean that much to you."

I think I already have. But of course, Greg did not voice his thoughts. "I'm glad you've found so much happiness, Patty. Look, the nurse is signaling that it's time for our visit. You go on in this time. When you come out, I'll be gone, but I'll be back within the two-hour interval."

Greg made his way to the pay phones at the end of the hall. He hoped someone would be home at the Burbank house. He wanted to let them know he was leaving the hospital now to pick up Danny and take him home for an hour. He wouldn't have time to wait around for him, so he wanted Danny to be ready to go.

He should have had the Burbanks' telephone number committed to memory by this time. Danny and Jimmy spent so much time together that theirs was a number he called frequently. But today Greg's brain was running on cruise control. He could barely remember his own name. He opened the phone book and made a note of the number, shoved some coins in the slots, and dialed.

After the seventh ring, he decided that no one was going to answer. His shoulders sagged with disappointment. He felt a strong need to be with his son, and he was sure Danny was feeling some of that same need.

There was nothing to do but to go home without him. After he showered, shaved, and put on clean clothes, he'd stop by the Burbank house on his way back to the hospital. Maybe by then they would have returned, and at least he could get a hug and a few quick words with his little boy.

Greg unlocked the front door and walked into his spacious

new house. Everything smelled new, even the wood and the walls. Everything had turned out just the way he had planned it, and yet the house seemed so cold and empty!

It wasn't just a scarcity of furniture that gave it that feel. He would take care of that in time. But there was no cheer in these rooms. Instead of radiating warmth, they looked like a page out of *Better Homes and Gardens*. Maybe when Greg's mother was well and strong and Danny came home to stay, things would be different in this house. But Greg knew the longing in his heart was for more than his mother and his child. As precious as they were to him, the deep emptiness in his heart would remain there until. . .

He moved up the stairs to his new bedroom where he had hung and arranged his clothes only a few days before. He pulled clean clothes from the dresser drawers. He was sure he would feel better once he had that shower.

❧

Thirty minutes later, Greg stood in front of a foggy bathroom mirror and ran his electric razor over the thick, dark stubble that covered his chin. He hadn't realized how terrible he looked! He fastened the last button of his clean shirt, pulled on his trousers, and stood in his stocking feet, wondering if he would be able to reach Danny by now.

He remembered his sister telling him he was supposed to call Tiffany too. He might as well do that first and get it over with here and now, where he had a shred of privacy. It was hard to carry on a private conversation on those hospital phones.

Tiffany answered on the second ring. "Tiffany here."

"Hello, Tiffany. It's Greg. I got your message, and—"

"Greg! You naughty, naughty boy! You haven't called me all week. Where have you been?"

"Look, Tiffany, my mother is in the hospital. She's been in a terrible automobile accident, and I—"

"Oooh, Darlin', that's just awful. Then I shall forgive you

this once. What hospital is she in?"

"She's in Martin Memorial. She's in the intensive care unit."

"I'm so sorry, Greg. I'll send her a get-well card right away. I know when I'm under the weather, cards always help to make me feel better."

Greg wanted to bring this senseless conversation to an end, to free up the line so he could call his son, but Tiffany babbled on. "The reason I've wanted to talk to you is to tell you the yacht club is throwing a big holiday gala in December, and I wanted to make sure you got our tickets in time. They're expecting a very large crowd, so do hurry, Greg, before they're sold out."

"Tiffany, I don't believe you heard a word I have said." He raised his pitch and spoke louder. "My mother is in intensive care, and you expect me to go out and buy tickets to some party? You must be out of your mind."

"Now, don't get upset, Darlin'. If you had listened to me, you'd realize the party isn't until the Christmas holidays. That's weeks away; surely your mother will be well by then. It's just that if we don't go ahead and get our tickets now—"

It took every bit of Greg's self-control to keep from screaming into the phone. He took great care to modulate his voice. "I'm very sorry, Tiffany. I'm sure that I won't be able to go to your party in December or whenever it is. In truth, I'm just not the partying type. I think you should call someone else to take you—someone who enjoys more of the same kinds of things that you do—because you and I just don't seem to be functioning on the same wavelength."

"Well!" Tiffany drew in a deep, audible breath. "I can certainly take a hint, Greg Cunningham. I'm not entirely stupid, you know!"

Well, you sure had me fooled about that! To his credit, Greg kept his sarcasm to himself. He was too much of a gentleman to do otherwise. "Look, Tiffany, I have to get back to the hospital now, but I do apologize if I've led you to expect more from me than I can deliver. Anyway, I wish you luck. Good-bye, Tiffany."

Tiffany was still ranting when he slid the receiver back onto its base. He felt sorry he had hurt her, but it was much better for both of them to have a clean break now before things went any further. And now his line was free to call his son.

This time his head was clear, and he remembered the number of the Burbank residence without looking it up. He dialed and prayed for a quick answer.

"Hello." He recognized Mary Burbank's voice.

"Mary, I can't tell you how much I appreciate your taking such good care of Danny for me. I know he's happy when he's with Jimmy. I've tried to keep him from worrying about his grandmother until we know what the outcome will be."

"How is she, Greg?" Mary's voice was tender and filled with sympathy. Although Greg had only known Mary and Herb Burbank for a few months, they had quickly become two of his closest friends, and Jimmy was like part of his family.

"We don't know much yet," he told her. "She's very critical." He related the facts as he knew them, and asked that the family continue to pray for her.

"You know we will, Greg. Reverend Hall has his prayer warriors working around the clock. What else can we do to help?"

"Letting Danny stay with you is the biggest help in the world, Mary. I don't worry about him when I know he's with you, and I know he's happy with the arrangement. Can I speak to him for a minute?"

His request was met with silence from the other end, so profound that Greg thought for a minute that his line had gone dead. "Mary? Are you still there?"

"Greg, isn't Danny with you?"

"What do you mean, Mary? You told me Herb was picking the boys up from school after they practiced for their Thanksgiving program. Didn't he bring him home with Jimmy?"

Greg's panic hit new limits as he completely lost control. He shouted into the phone, *"Mary, don't do this to me! Where is my son?"*

Herb Burbank took the telephone from his wife. "Hold on, Greg. I'm sure Danny's all right. There must be a logical explanation for this. When I went to pick up the boys at school this afternoon, Jimmy came out alone and told me you were picking up Danny. He said Danny told him you were coming to get him, and that you'd be by to pick up his stuff later. I should have checked, I guess, but I've never known either of the boys to lie. That's why I'm sure it's just some kind of a mix-up. Danny probably went home with someone else. I'm going back to the school right now. We'll get to the bottom of this."

"I'll meet you there," Greg said tersely. His blood had turned to ice water, and his whole body had begun to shake. *Danny.* His son Danny was missing!

eighteen

By the time Libby pulled out of the hospital driveway and turned onto the main drag, daylight was fading and dusk was beginning to fall. She considered waiting until tomorrow to finish her work at Blue Dolphin, but she couldn't do that. The calls on her desk were all from people who depended on her, and although their needs were probably not as urgent as her own, she felt a responsibility to them.

Her first priority was to check on Celia. She felt a twinge of guilt as she remembered she was supposed to be caring for her sister, making sure she rested and didn't overdo it.

As soon as she talked to Celia and took care of any immediate needs, she'd run out to the deli and pick up some baked chicken for their supper. She could microwave some frozen vegetables and toss a salad for Celia, and have her own meal later after she finished her work at the office.

Having settled that, she drove directly home. Seeing Bob Jennings's car beside the curb brought a big smile to Libby's face. That man must have been heaven-sent! She should have known he would make sure Celia had whatever she needed. *Thank you, Lord, for sending this kind man into our lives.*

She parked her car in the drive and hurried up the front steps. "I'm home, Celia. Sorry I've neglected you today."

To Libby's surprise, Celia was dressed in her prettiest frock. Was that rosy glow on her face acquired by makeup, or was it just her happiness showing its color? "My, don't you look nice."

Bob sat on the sofa while Celia stood to greet her sister with a hug. "Go get dressed yourself. Bob wants to take us both out to dinner tonight. Oh, it feels so good to be getting dressed up to go out again."

Relief spread through Libby's tired body. "That's great, Celia. You two go ahead without me. I have some work to catch up on at the office, and I'll grab a bite to eat on the way home."

Celia looked shocked. "You're not going back to work tonight, are you, Libby? Look what time it is! Please say you'll go with us. We both want you to, don't we, Bob?"

"Indeed we do." But seeing the determined set to Libby's chin, he offered a compromise. "If you really must go back to the office tonight, Libby, we'll bring you a carryout dinner from the restaurant. That way you won't have to stop anywhere on the way home, and maybe we'll all meet here later and have dessert together."

Thankful to be let off the hook, Libby aimed a smile of appreciation at Bob. "That's a wonderful idea. I'll put on the coffee as soon as I get home. You two take your time and enjoy your meal, and I'll see you later this evening."

Although Celia looked dubious about the plan, Libby gave her a quick kiss and went out the door before her sister could voice any more objections.

By the time she reached Blue Dolphin Drive, a slight drizzle had begun to fall and there was a chill in the air. Libby slid her card into the automatic gate and parked in front of the administration building.

Although the administration building itself was dark, electric streetlights cast a faint glow over the area and made the grass glisten as though it were sprinkled with tiny chips of emeralds. But what was that bundle on the stoop? Libby tried to remember if the office was scheduled for any kind of delivery that day, but she drew a blank. They never allowed deliveries after closing because the gate would be locked. Yet she hadn't seen a package by the door when she left here earlier. If it had been there, she would have surely tripped over it. Someone within the Blue Dolphin complex must have left something there for her.

She approached the steps with cautious curiosity. She had read some strange stories in the papers lately about bombs that were placed to hurt innocent people. But surely nothing like that could happen at Blue Dolphin, could it? Admittedly, she seemed to have a few enemies lately, but not any of that extreme.

She stopped just short of the steps and was about to back away and look for help when an amazing thing happened. The bundle moved! It contained something alive!

"Miss Libby? Is that you, Miss Libby?"

"Danny? Danny Cunningham!" As the little boy unfolded and stretched, Libby could hardly believe what she was seeing. "What on earth are you doing here at this hour? Why, your clothes are soaking wet. Get inside before you catch your death of cold."

Libby's hands shook as she manipulated her key in the lock and pushed the front door open. Danny struggled to his feet and stumbled over the threshold.

Libby had so many questions she didn't know which one to ask first. "Danny, are you all right? How did you get here?"

His teeth were chattering so badly that his lips could not form an answer. Libby took off her own sweater and wrapped it around his shoulders. "Let me fix you something hot to drink. I think Lorraine has some tea bags over here." She filled a mug with water and put it in the microwave. When the water was hot, she added an herbal tea bag and a heaping spoonful of sugar. "Here, drink this, and then tell me how you got here."

He looked up at her as though the answer should be obvious. "I walked."

"From where? From your grandmother's condo?"

"No, Ma'am. . .from school. See, I didn't know it was this far when I started out. It never seemed this far when I rode the bus. Miss Libby, you told me one time I could come here to talk to you whenever I felt like it, and I sure did feel like it today." Tears ran down his cheeks and mixed with rainwater. Libby thought her heart would break for him.

She grabbed a stack of towels from the bathroom and handed them to him. "Take off your wet jacket and dry your hair, Danny. Wrap some of these towels around you and start at the beginning. Tell me what's wrong."

Danny did as he was told, sniffling and wiping his nose on the back of his hands until Libby gave him a box of tissues from Lorraine's desk. "Just about everything is wrong. Do you know about my grandma?"

"Yes, Danny. I know about her accident, and I'm very sorry. Is that why you're so upset? You're worried about her?"

"Yeah, I reckon that's a big part of it. But like I told you before, nobody ever tells me nothin'. Is Grandma dead?"

"Oh, no, Danny." She put her arms around him and snuggled him to her bosom. "Your grandmother is fighting very hard to get better. And we can all help by praying for her." But then another thought occurred to Libby. "Doesn't anyone know where you are? Your father must be frantic with worry."

"No, he won't be worried, 'cause he hasn't had time to think about me lately. He thinks I'm at Jimmy's, an' I told Jimmy I was goin' with my dad. I'm sorry about the lie, Miss Libby. I know lyin' is wrong, but I just had to see you, and I couldn't think of any other way."

She continued to hold him close as she tried to plan what she should do. "Danny, we have to let people know where you are. That's the first thing we must do, and after that, we can talk things over." She picked up the phone and dialed some numbers. First she tried Greg's number, knowing he would not likely be at home. Then it occurred to her that this was Greg's old number and would ring in his mother's condominium. Sure enough, after a few rings, the answering machine came on. "Sorry I can't come to the phone right now, but if you'll leave your number and a brief message, I'll get back to you as soon as I can."

Not having any other immediate options, Libby left a message explaining that Danny was with her, and that he was safe. Perhaps Patty would come back out to the condo, or Greg might call his machine to retrieve his messages.

"Danny, do you know the telephone number of the people where you've been staying? Who have you been visiting?"

"Jimmy," he said. "I don't know his number. At my grandma's condo, Dad put it on the automatic dial so I only had to punch number twelve when I wanted to talk to Jimmy."

Libby felt frustration creeping in, but she tried to remain calm. "Do you know Jimmy's last name? What's his father's name?"

At last Danny supplied the necessary information so Libby could look up the number and dial the Burbank residence. A frantic voice answered after the first ring. "Yes?"

"Mrs. Burbank?"

"Yes. But if you're calling to advertise a product, I must ask you to keep this line open for an emergency call." Mary spoke so quickly that Libby knew she was eager to break the connection.

"No, wait," Libby said. "Please don't hang up. I have important information concerning Danny Cunningham. Are you his—"

"Danny? You know where he is? Is he all right? Oh, please tell me he's safe."

Libby could hear the anguish in Mrs. Burbank's voice. "Danny is fine," she assured her. "He's here with me at the Blue Dolphin Condominium office. I'll let you talk to him in just a moment, but please don't scold him. He's tired and confused right now, and he just needs a little extra reassurance." Libby handed the telephone to Danny. "Here, Danny. Talk to Jimmy's mother and let her know you're okay. Then we'll have time to talk while we wait for someone to come for you."

Danny's conversation with Mary Burbank was brief, consisting mostly of yes ma'ams and no ma'ams, and then he handed the phone back to Libby. "Don't worry about him, Mrs. Burbank. Danny will be safe here with me until someone comes to pick him up."

"I have to hang up right away," Mary said. "I must get word to Greg as soon as I can. He's absolutely beside himself with worry." Without waiting for a reply, the woman hung up, leaving Libby holding a dead line. But Libby understood completely why it was necessary to end the conversation abruptly. Evidently Greg knew Danny was missing. He would be absolutely insane with worry.

Libby pressed a button on the office wall that raised the automatic gate and locked it in the open position. Whoever came for Danny could drive right up to the office without waiting for assistance.

"Now, Danny, let's talk about what's wrong. I've told you your grandmother is in the hospital where the doctors and nurses are trying to help her get better. What else is on your mind?"

"Is Grandma gonna die?" New tears poured down his freckled cheeks.

"Now, Danny, no one but God knows when anyone will be called to live in heaven. But your dad and your aunt Patty have been praying for her, and so have I."

"Me too, an' Jimmy's family too. I hope God says it's okay for Grandma to stay down here longer. I don't want her to go to heaven yet."

"We're all asking God for that, Danny. Now we have to trust God to do what is best for everyone. Is that the only thing that brought you here today?"

"Well. . .no. . .see, I just keep askin' questions like when is my dad gonna take me home, or when is my grandma gonna get better, or why doesn't my dad come by here to see me. You know, stuff like that."

"Well, what do they tell you when you ask?" From her brief conversation with Mary Burbank, Libby was sure she was a kind Christian mother who would go to all extremes to avoid hurting Danny.

"They just try to get me to think about somethin' else. Like Jimmy's mom keeps bakin' me special cookies an' playin' games with us. Whenever I try to talk about Grandma or anything like that, they just try to change the subject." Danny snuggled up against Libby's side, and Libby was glad to note his trembling had stopped. He seemed much calmer and more relaxed.

"I guess they're just trying to keep you from worrying, Danny. But I understand what you're saying. You'd rather just have them come out and talk to you about it so you know what's going on. Right?"

"Right. Nobody talks to me like you do. That's why I had to come here. But see, I thought I'd get here before you left work. I didn't know it was so far. I walked an' walked, and then it started to rain, an' it got dark, an' I got scared. When I got here an' you were gone, I didn't know what to do. I just laid down on the steps, an' I was cryin', an' I guess I musta gone to sleep, 'cause the next thing I knew, you was here an' I knew everything was gonna be okay."

Libby wondered what she had ever done to inspire such devotion. But there were serious problems yet to face. "Danny, can you imagine how worried your dad must have been when he learned you were missing?"

"Well, I figured he had kinda turned me over to the Burbanks. He's got a lotta things on his mind. The new house, an' Tiffany, an' now Grandma, so I didn't think he'd even know I was gone. An' I didn't want Jimmy's mom and dad to worry, so that's why I made up the lie. That was bad, wasn't it?"

"Telling the truth is always the best way, Danny. It can really save a lot of trouble. But now we just have to deal with things as they are. Someone will be coming here soon to get you, but I want you to know I'm glad you feel you can talk to me. I'm going to write my telephone number on this card so you can call me, and we can talk any time you feel like it. Okay?"

"Wow, Miss Libby. You're really great."

As Libby's eyes welled with tears, headlights beamed through the front office windows and a car door slammed. Heavy footsteps sounded on the walk. "Danny?" It was Greg!

nineteen

The emotional reunion between father and son should be private, Libby decided. They would not need a third party watching. "Danny, go unlock the front door and let your dad come in." Libby eased herself into her own office and closed the door.

Although her mind was elsewhere, she picked up the list of calls she promised to make and started dialing. Occasionally, between calls, she could hear muffled noises from the front office, sometimes a laugh or a giggle, but she made a conscientious effort to concentrate on her own affairs.

Thirty minutes later, she had completed her calls and was putting her notes away when she heard a timid knock on her door. "Come in. It's not locked."

When the door opened, she thought her heart would burst with joy at the sight of the two of them. Wide smiles spread across their faces, and their eyes, though puffy and red, sparkled with love and happiness. Both of them surrounded her at once and wrapped their arms around her.

Then, releasing her, Greg was the first to speak. "Thank you for being here for Danny when he needed you, Libby. How is it you always seem to be at the right place at the right time?"

"It might seem to be a piece of good luck that I came out here tonight," Libby said, "but I choose to think things happen for a reason. God had His hand in this tonight, I am sure." She tousled Danny's hair with her fingers. His red locks, now dry, had sprung in all directions and reminded Libby of a field of sprouting alfalfa.

And Greg, for all his harried appearance, had never looked

more appealing. She longed to throw her arms around his neck and feel his cheek next to hers. But of course, there would always be Tiffany.

She couldn't deny now that she loved Greg, and Danny too. Knowing there could never be anything more than friendship between them, she would have to make sure her feelings did not ever show.

"Danny's going back to spend the night with Jimmy tonight," Greg said. "He feels all right about that now that we've talked. And he told me how much you helped him understand." The look in his eyes expressed more gratitude than words ever could.

"I'm going back to the hospital as soon as I get Danny settled," Greg continued. "Are you coming back there tonight?" His voice was like a plea.

As much as she wanted to go, to be with him and offer whatever comfort she could, she knew he did not really need her there anymore. Patty was there, and probably Tiffany too, and she would just be excess baggage. As impossible as it seemed, she had to make herself forget him somehow. This was probably the best time to make that break.

"I can't tonight, Greg. I have some things at home that need to be taken care of, and. . .um. . .I'm expecting company a little later." She slung her purse over her shoulder and edged toward the front door. "If you and Danny are ready to move on, I'd better lock this place up and be on my way."

"Of course. Come on, Danny." Greg's shoulders sagged with all the burdens heaped on them this night, and Libby had to turn her head away to keep from changing her mind.

❧

A phone rang in the distance, and Libby roused herself from a deep sleep. No, the sound was not distant at all—it only sounded that way because her head was buried in her pillow. The phone was ringing quite close and it was *her* phone. But it was barely light outside.

She squinted at her alarm clock and then jumped out of bed. Six o'clock! Who would be calling so early? She reached the phone on its fifth ring. Breathlessly, she answered, "Hello?"

"Libby. I'm sorry if I woke you up, but I wanted to be sure I caught you before you left for the office."

Fearing the worst, Libby sank onto a chair. "What is it, Greg? How is she?"

"Patty and I have just talked to the doctors. I had to call you first, Libby, because we've just received that miracle we've been praying for." His enthusiasm carried over the line. She could picture him standing at the phone, wearing that sweet, dimpled smile she had grown to love.

"Your mother is better? Tell me what is happening."

"Well, Mom opened her eyes and tried to talk to us last night. Of course, she couldn't with that tube down her throat. Her vital signs had improved so much that even the doctors were calling it a miracle. And as soon as they took her off the respirator, all she could say was, 'I'm hungry.' "

"Oh, Greg, I'm so happy for all of you. I'll pass the word around Blue Dolphin when I get to work this morning. This will be a cause for celebration."

"Actually, Libby, another reason I called so early was to see if you'd swing by the hospital on your way to work and have breakfast with me in the cafeteria. There are still some things I want to say to you."

It would be so easy to take the little bit he was offering, even simple friendship, but Libby knew she would only be setting herself up for future heartbreak. She had to be strong. "I–I'd really like to, Greg, but I never did finish everything I had to do last night, and I think I'll try to get to the office pretty early today."

The silence on the other end of the line compelled her to continue. "I'm so very glad about your mother's improvement. I'll keep praying for her."

"Thanks," he said, but she could hear his disappointment.

"Actually, that was one of the reasons I wanted you to come this morning. Remember when we went to the chapel to pray for her?"

"Of course I remember." Libby would never forget the intimacy she felt in that moment, in the presence of Jesus with Greg by her side.

"Well," Greg continued, "I just thought it would be appropriate for us to go back and thank Him for answering our prayer in such a wonderful way."

Libby felt a chill run through her body. That was such an incredibly beautiful thought. If only she and Greg—but no, she must not let herself even dream of such an impossibility.

"I'm sorry, Greg. I can't come, but I'll thank Him right here from my home. And thank you so much for sharing with me this morning."

"Right. Well then, I'll be seeing you, Libby. Take care of yourself."

"Give my love to Patty, and to Danny too." *But most of all, to you, Greg. I wish I could tell you how I feel.* Libby replaced the receiver and wiped a tear from each eye.

❧

Libby had barely begun her day when everything seemed to happen at once. First, there was the visit from Michael Phillips.

"Lorraine just told me the good news about Lenore Cunningham. Our little complex certainly has rallied around to support her and her family." He pulled a chair close to her desk so that he sat facing her, and his grim countenance warned her that he had come here to talk about more than Mrs. Cunningham.

"Libby," he began, "I've met with the board of directors. They want to schedule a meeting on Friday and get this manager thing settled once and for all. And I can't see any point in dragging things out."

"No," Libby agreed. "I'd like to know where I stand."

"Well, I just wanted an opportunity to sit down with you before Friday, to let you know your work here has been exemplary. I hope you'll be our property manager for a long, long time. But in the event that things don't work out the way we both want them to, you can count on me to relocate you or to give you the finest letter of recommendation that I am capable of composing."

"I—I appreciate that, Michael. I know these last few weeks have been hard for you too, and I'm glad things will soon settle down to a normal routine."

Libby was surprised when her intercom buzzer sounded. Lorraine never interrupted her when she and Michael were in conference unless the matter was one of extreme urgency. "Yes?"

"Libby, there's a man on the phone, a Mr. Chandler from the blood bank, and I think you should talk to him."

Libby punched the button to connect with the blinking line. "Good morning, Mr. Chandler. How can I help you?"

"Miss Malone, this is a bit unusual, but I want to ask your permission to send out a mobile unit to collect blood from your condominium community today. You see, we've had many people call in who want to donate blood for Lenore Cunningham, and they insist on doing so immediately. We do appreciate their offers, and we don't want to miss any of them because our supplies at the blood bank have been critically low lately."

"Why, yes, Mr. Chandler. You can set up right outside our clubhouse. What time would you like to come?"

Michael Phillips gave her a questioning look, but she held up a finger to delay her explanation.

"Yes, ten o'clock will be fine, Mr. Chandler. What was that last thing you said?"

"Just that we processed two of your donors last night because they had the type of blood that matches Mrs. Cunningham's. Let's see, there was a Mrs. Viola Paschal and a

Mr. Adam Ridgefield. The others we will collect at ten o'clock."

When she finished the call, she explained to Michael. "And at least one of the donors might surprise you. Selena's nephew Adam Ridgefield has the O-negative blood type that Lenore needs. He went to the blood bank last night, along with Mrs. Paschal, that new lady in building 184. She and her husband just moved in last month, so I doubt she even knows Mrs. Cunningham. Isn't it amazing how these people come together to help each other in times of need? Just like one big family!"

"And yet they'll squabble like cats and dogs when things don't suit them," Michael said. "But I guess that's life. We all like to have things going our own way, but the closeness of condominium life demands understanding and compromise."

"It's a matter of give-and-take, isn't it?"

"Yes, Libby, and you're one of the givers. Now if I have my way about this, you'll be one of the takers too."

He got up to leave. "About Friday, Libby. . ."

"Yes?"

"Good luck!"

twenty

At last the day of reckoning had arrived. The board of directors of Blue Dolphin began to assemble for the special meeting to decide whether Libby Malone would be offered the permanent position of on-site manager of Blue Dolphin, or whether other candidates should be considered for the job.

Libby sat in the back of the room to listen and learn her fate. She was sure the decision had already been made, and that this meeting was a mere formality to confirm her worst fears.

Seated at the head table, Selena Watson clutched the microphone front and center, a grim, determined set to her prominent chin. She was flanked on either side by Mark Garrity, the vice president, and Melissa Resmondo, the secretary. At one end of the table sat Charles Williams, the treasurer, clutching his ledger. Michael Phillips sat at the other end, looking pale and somber.

Selena rapped her gavel and called the meeting to order. "Since this is not a regularly scheduled meeting, we will dispense with the normal business routine and get right down to the matter we have come here to discuss. We are to decide whether to offer the permanent job of on-site property manager to Libby Malone who has been our *assistant* manager for the past two years, or to advertise and actively recruit other candidates who might be better qualified to fill this role.

"I will give you my thoughts on this in a moment, but first I would like to know if any of you in the audience would care to express an opinion before your board casts its final vote."

From the rear of the room, a hand shot up and Selena

addressed the elderly gentleman. "Would you please step up to the microphone and introduce yourself, Sir? I'm sure we'd all like to hear what you have to say."

The man made his way to the front of the room and blew into the mike to make sure it was connected. Hearing a satisfying blast of air reverberate through the room, he began to speak. "My name is Abner Goforth, and I got no quarrel with Libby Malone nor anyone else, for that matter. But I said it before and I'll say it again. Management is a man's job. Any good God-fearing woman ought to be home cooking and keeping her house in order, and I say we need a man to run our condominium affairs."

At least thirty angry women rose to their feet at once, loudly voicing their protests, until Selena was forced to rap her gavel to restore order. "Thank you for your opinion, Mr. Goforth. Now, who would like to be heard next?"

Several people stood at once, but quickly reclaimed their seats when they saw a young gentleman stride toward the microphone with a very purposeful look on his face. Libby saw him too, and her heart seemed to lurch all the way up into her throat. *What is Greg Cunningham doing at this meeting?*

He gripped the microphone and looked at Selena. "Madam President," he began, "I know I have no right to speak at your meeting because I am not a property owner here, nor am I even a resident. But I have a few things I'd like to say to these good people, and I hope you'll give me that opportunity."

"This is highly irregular, Mr. Cunningham. This is a private meeting, and you have no voice in the matter we have come here to discuss."

"I know that, Mrs. Watson. But what I have to say is important to the people who live here, and—"

Selena rapped her gavel. "Please, Mr. Cunningham. I must ask you to leave. You have no business even being here with us today."

"Hold on, Selena." It was Mark Garrity, the vice president, who spoke out. Even without a microphone, his voice carried throughout the room and drew immediate attention. "I don't see what harm it can do to hear what this man has to say. We don't have to be so formal that we can't bend a rule now and then."

"I agree," Melissa Resmondo said. "He's not asking to vote or anything, Selena. His mother is a resident whom we've all known for a long time. We know why she isn't able to be present today, so I think out of respect to Lenore Cunningham, we should listen to what her son has to say."

Libby saw the hint of a smile on Michael Phillips's lips. She knew he was powerless to express his opinion at this meeting, but his feelings were written all over his face.

Selena scowled. "It looks like I am outvoted by my own board. Well, just let me warn you. If you aren't careful, before you know it, we'll be having everybody on the street coming in here wanting to tell us how to run our association."

"Oh, I don't think it will come to that, Selena," Mark said calmly. "Go ahead, Greg. Let us hear what's on your mind."

Greg nodded his thanks to Mark and turned to the audience. "I want to begin by thanking you as a group for the outpouring of love and support you have given to me during my mother's illness. Your attitude has literally changed my life forever. But before I tell you about that, I want to apologize to you."

A hush fell over the room as Greg's eyes wandered back and forth over his audience, leaving no doubt as to his sincerity.

"When I first came here to Blue Dolphin to stay in my mother's condo for a few weeks, I had a very hard time accepting some of your rules. Through the help of a good friend, I learned why these rules are necessary, and I learned to make some difficult adjustments and compromises, just as all of you had to do when you moved from your former homes into a congregate living situation."

Nods and murmurs from the audience revealed that many of them understood about the difficulty of changing their lifestyles.

"But my apology goes beyond that," Greg continued. "I am embarrassed now to admit that I had foolishly formed an opinion that stereotyped you folks, based solely on your age. And if you're honest, I think some of you will realize you did the same thing with me in the beginning.

"But this same friend who helped me understand about the necessity of your rules also opened my eyes to the fact that we are all human beings created by God, just trying to get along together in the same world. Age and gender have little to do with our temperaments or the makeup of our personalities.

"My entire outlook on life has changed since spending those few weeks among you. I have learned that being a Christian extends way beyond attending services on Sunday, or even studying the Bible. The love and support you folks have shown me here at Blue Dolphin is the Christlike kind of love that recognizes neither age nor gender, and it is the most vivid example I have ever seen of true Christian spirit. For this priceless gift, I want to thank you from the bottom of my heart.

"I suppose by now most of you have guessed that the good friend who helped me open my eyes to see all of this is your interim property manager, Libby Malone. And if you folks let Libby get away from you, well, you're not as smart as I think you are.

"That's all I have to say, and I thank you for letting me express my feelings here today. Allowing me this privilege was just another example of your generosity and understanding."

As Greg turned away from the microphone and walked toward the back door, the room shook with thunderous applause. Over half the audience stood. Amid all the noise, one small lady made her way to the microphone. Libby recognized elderly Mrs. Frierson, the lady who at the last meeting had precariously teetered on a chair to avoid Danny's pet frog. And helping her push her way through the crowd was Mr. Gabbard who had risen to her rescue. Libby held her breath and cringed, waiting to hear a recount of that fateful day when everything seemed to go wrong at once.

Mr. Gabbard positioned the lady in front of the microphone and stood beside her, holding her elbow for support. Mrs. Frierson fiddled with a hearing aid in her left ear before she spoke. "I don't hear so good, but I thought I heard that young man say something about letting Libby get away from us. Why would she want to do that? Doesn't she like us anymore?"

While Mr. Gabbard leaned over and spoke directly into her right ear, summing up the situation for her in a few words, Selena Watson interrupted. "Mrs. Frierson, let me explain to you what all of this is about. Here at Blue Dolphin, we have had nothing but problems lately, and you of all people should understand what I mean. Why, Mrs. Frierson, don't you recall the problem we had at the last meeting when a—a creature was allowed to enter the clubhouse and nearly caused you to have a heart attack?"

"That wasn't a creature," the old lady snapped. "That was a plain old toad frog. And of course it scared me. We can't have frogs in the clubhouse—it's against the rules. But I don't see what that has to do with Libby leaving us. She's our friend. We can't let her go away."

Again the crowd was on its feet, applauding Mrs. Frierson's words. Mr. Gabbard leaned into the mike, but his eyes met Selena's. "I guess the board knows how we feel about this matter—most of us at least. Now let's all sit down and listen to them take their vote."

Selena's face was almost as red as her carefully lacquered fingernails. "Well," she said, "I will call for a vote from the board, but not before I express my own opinion. I have nothing personal against Miss Malone, but I have watched her carefully over the last few weeks, and I have observed absenteeism and a flagrant disregard for our rules. I believe a change is in order at this time. Now, I have served as your president for the past four years, and if you want me to continue serving you, I'd like a show of support from my board."

The room was ominously quiet. Finally Mark Garrity spoke softly into the microphone. "Selena, you know we all appreciate what you've done for us over the years, and I for one hope you will continue to work with us on the board. But it's not fair to expect one person to carry so much of the burden alone. Sometimes a rotation of officers can spell relief for the overworked, and even serve to strengthen a healthy organization."

Selena pushed her chair away from the table and stood with her hands on her hips. "Are you asking for my resignation, Mark? Because if you are. . ."

"Sit down, Selena," Charles Williams ordered sternly. "Nobody has asked for anything. We came here to attend to a specific business matter, and I suggest we stick to the subject and cast our votes."

Libby slipped behind the last row of chairs and headed for the exit. She did not want to be present when the vote was taken, and besides that, she hoped to catch up with Greg before he drove away. No matter how the board voted, she owed him a vote of thanks for what he tried to do for her. She would always remember the sweet things he said about her, and she would cherish his words in her heart forever.

She almost tripped in her haste to catch him. He was just backing out of his parking space when he saw her and stopped. He leaned over and opened the passenger door for her. "Get in and I'll give you a lift to wherever you are going."

Libby climbed into the front seat and pulled the door closed after her. The nearness of him was almost more than she could bear. "Thanks, Greg. I was hoping to catch you before you got away. I wanted to thank you for what you tried to do for me." The clean, woodsy masculine scent that was so typically Greg made her pulse quicken, but she kept her voice light and impersonal.

"No thanks necessary, Libby. I just spoke the words from my heart. But I've been wondering about something. Now that I'm no longer a Blue Dolphin resident, don't you think you might reconsider our friendship, and let us start all over from the beginning?"

Libby's pulse was racing at an alarming speed. Wasn't this exactly what she had hoped for? And yet, when Greg had uttered the word "friendship," it had pierced her heart like a sharp-pointed arrow.

She had forced herself to accept the fact that Greg was in love with someone else. She was grateful to Danny for telling her about Tiffany before she had made a complete fool of herself. But friendship? Could she accept a simple friendship with Greg, knowing her heart longed for so much more?

"You're very quiet, Libby. Is it so hard for you to decide to let me be your friend?"

"Oh, no. It's not that at all, Greg. It's just that—well, you're going to be very busy getting settled into your new home, and with your wedding coming up. . ."

"My what? How did you know I'm thinking of getting married? Are you clairvoyant or what?" His lips twitched as he tried in vain to restrain a smile.

Seeing his familiar grin and feeling the warmth of his body so close to her own, Libby's heart ached so that she could scarcely bear it. "It's not a matter of clairvoyance, Greg. But I'm afraid Danny let the cat out of the bag. I hope you won't scold him for sharing your little secret, but he told me about Tiffany a couple of weeks ago."

"Tiffany? Danny told you about Tiffany? What did he tell you? That he dislikes her with a passion?" Greg's grin turned to a look of puzzlement. "What's Tiffany got to do with my thoughts of marriage?"

"Well, aren't you—I mean, Danny said—" Libby felt herself

coming apart at the seams. She had struggled so hard to put up an impassive front, but the battle was lost almost before it began.

Greg pulled his car over to the side of the road, and in broad daylight with all the world watching, he pulled Libby into his arms and let her release the long pent-up tears on his shoulder. "Libby, Darling, I don't know what Danny told you, but there is only one woman in the world that I hope to marry, and I am holding her right here in my arms."

Libby looked up through teary eyes to see if Greg could possibly be serious. Was he teasing her again? But the look on his face told her everything she wanted to know. "Greg Cunningham, is this a proposal?"

"Yes, and a very honorable one. Libby, if you will be my wife, I promise to cherish you forever, for as long as God grants us our time together here on earth. And you will make both Danny and me the two happiest men in the whole wide world."

Libby reached up and pulled his face down to hers. "Put like that, how could I refuse?"

Greg's face almost glowed with joy. He lowered his lips to hers, and they sealed their sacred promise with a kiss.

twenty-one

Crowds of people dressed in their Sunday best streamed into the Blue Dolphin clubhouse while the musicians tuned up their instruments to play romantic tunes of the forties. It was the first big social event since Libby Malone had been officially named as property manager of the Blue Dolphin, and not one single resident wanted to miss it.

Patty checked the punch table to make sure there were enough cups. "Did you really expect this many people to show up?" she asked Libby. "Do all of them live here in Blue Dolphin?"

"Most of them do," Libby told her. "We invited the entire community, and most of them love a party, especially when it has an element of surprise. Your mother had the invitations distributed, but Greg did the wording and had them printed. Did you see one of them?"

"Yes, they were beautiful. He called this a "Welcome Home Party for Lenore Cunningham." But I especially liked the wording he used that said, "This is our way of saying 'thanks' to all of you for your love and support through the long weeks of my mother's recuperation."

"He's very charged up about this party," Libby admitted, "and so am I. It's going to be a special evening for us to remember." Libby looked radiant in a simple sheath dress of pale yellow silk. Her brown eyes sparkled with excitement.

"I know Mom is as happy as a clam, and proud too. But what's this about a surprise? I heard several people asking about the cryptic message printed at the bottom of the invitation. *Do you like surprises?* it asks. Then it goes on to say, *If you do, you won't want to miss this one!* Do you know what that brother of mine has up his sleeve?"

Libby beamed a secret smile. "It's more fun if we just speculate for a while. We'd better hope he's not planning to let Danny release another frog in the clubhouse." She winked at Patty, whose blank expression reminded Libby that Greg's sister would have no way of knowing what she was referring to.

Patty did not pursue the issue of frogs. "Speaking of Danny, where is my favorite nephew?"

"He went with Greg to pick up the cake. Technically speaking, the party hasn't even begun yet, but these people were so eager to come that they all showed up a half hour early."

"Then we'd better put the ice in this punch bowl and get things started," Patty said and took off for the kitchen.

Lenore, who was still not strong enough to stand for long periods of time, had been given a place of honor at the head table. Friends clustered around her in a circle, and others lined up for a turn to welcome her back to good health.

Libby thought she looked like a queen in her new lace dress. The soft delphinium blue accented the blond highlights of her perfectly coiffed hair. "She's never looked lovelier than she does tonight," Patty declared, as she ladled heart-shaped strawberry ice cubes into the punch bowl.

Libby went to the kitchen to see if the caterers had arrived yet and bumped headlong into Danny. "Oh, my goodness. I thought you went with your dad to get the cake."

"I did. We just got back. Look at it, Libby! Isn't it cool?"

Libby turned around and saw the huge cake, which was indeed "cool," and standing beside it, almost bursting with pride, was the dearest man in the whole world. "Greg, it's gorgeous!"

"So are you, Libby. You look ravishing." His eyes caressed her tenderly. He crossed the kitchen in a few long strides and kissed her on the lips, unmindful of the curious bystanders. "Come on. We need to get out of here so the caterers can get to work. They've assured me they'll take care of everything, if we'll just go out and leave them alone."

Greg led her to the table where his sister stood pouring sparkling pink fruit punch into clear glass cups. "It's quite delicious," she boasted, handing them each a cup. "I made it myself."

"Uh-oh!" Greg teased. "Well, we'll just have to drink some of it anyway."

Cups in hand, they made their way to the head table and claimed chairs beside Lenore. "Mom, can I get you a cup of punch?" Greg asked.

"No thank you, Darling. Danny just brought me one."

A momentary flash of alarm washed over Greg's face. "He didn't spill any of it, I hope."

"Not enough to worry about," Lenore assured him. "These cups don't hold very much, and grandmothers don't take much notice of a few little spills here and there."

Libby had no sooner sat down than she bounced up again. "Look, Greg. Here come Celia and Bob. Don't they make a striking couple?" She edged through the crowd to welcome them and invited them to join her at the head table.

Celia glowed with happiness, and Bob's adoration of her was no secret to anyone who happened to be watching.

Amid the chatter and merriment, all the guests eventually found seats at the tables, and Greg rose to address the crowd. Silence fell over the room as he spoke. "As you know, I wanted to give this party tonight to honor my mother, but also to honor each one of you, her friends. You have given unselfishly of your time and your love. You have sent enough delicious food to keep my mother, my sister, my son, and me well fed for the next six months. Thank goodness for freezers!" A wave of laughter echoed across the room. "And many of you have even donated your blood so that my mother could regain her strength and be with us here today. For all of this, and for all of you, my family and I will be eternally grateful. Now, let us bow in thanks to God, who has so richly blessed us."

As heads were bowed, Greg's deep rich voice carried throughout the room. When he pronounced the "Amen," he followed it by saying, "Please enjoy!" Then he sat down and picked up his fork.

"Wait a minute," a lady chirped from across the room. Libby recognized the voice of Mrs. Frierson. *What's she up to this time?*

"What is it?" Greg asked, rising to his feet again. "Did I forget something?"

"The surprise. You promised us a surprise," Mrs. Frierson challenged.

"Yes, I did," Greg admitted. "The surprise is yet to come. You might say that it will be your dessert." His mischievous grin spread across his face as he reclaimed his seat and began to eat.

Leaning across the table, Patty chided him. "Greg, that's mean. We are all waiting for the surprise. Is it really only something to eat?" She sounded a tiny bit disappointed, as though she had hoped for something entirely different.

"Just like everyone else, Patty, you'll have to wait and see."

At last the meal was over. As the waiters began to place servings of tiramisu before each guest, Patty exclaimed, "What a truly elegant-looking dessert, Greg. So this is the surprise! It really was something to eat after all." Again, Libby detected a hint of disappointment in her voice. "But what about that beautiful cake?"

"I came prepared," he explained. "I have a supply of Styrofoam boxes in the kitchen. Libby and I are going to send everyone home with a piece of our cake. He rose to his feet and tapped his fork against a glass to capture the audience's attention. "About that surprise," he began, and an immediate hush fell over the room. "Please share in my joy when I tell you that Libby Malone has consented to be my wife." He pulled Libby to her feet and kissed her while the guests cheered and clapped.

Mrs. Frierson offered the only objection. "Does this mean she's going to leave us after all?" She whined in a voice loud enough for all to hear. "Are you going to take her away from us?"

Greg and Libby both laughed, shaking their heads in denial, but Libby spoke the words of assurance everyone waited to hear. "I'm not going anywhere! I'll continue to be your property manager for as long as you'll have me. Of course, you know I'm gaining not only a husband but a son as well." She winked at Danny, who grinned back at her. "I'll be needing to spend more time at home now, so I won't be able to put in as many hours as I have in the past. But your president, Selena Watson, has graciously come up with a solution to help me work things out. Her nephew, Adam Ridgefield, will begin training as my assistant, and at least one of us will be on hand to help you whenever you need us."

That idea seemed to satisfy Mrs. Frierson, who sat down and attacked her dessert with gusto.

Libby and Greg circled the head table, accepting hugs and handshakes, and even a few tears. When Libby embraced her future mother-in-law, Greg could not resist the chance to needle her. "Mom, you missed out on this one completely. With all your skill at matchmaking, how does it happen you never thought of Libby for my future wife?"

"Oh, I did, Son. You still haven't realized it, but I orchestrated this whole thing."

"Yeah, right!" Greg said with a skeptical raise of his eyebrows. "Mom, you weren't even in the state. You'll have to admit you had nothing to do with this."

"That's what you think. I've had my eye on Libby for a couple of years now. I always knew she'd be the perfect wife for you."

Libby shook with laughter. "Now, Mrs. Cunningham." It was obvious that she too doubted Lenore could have had any part in the matchup.

Greg knew he had found his precious jewel all by himself, and he was not about to let his mother get away with stealing his limelight. "Then tell me this, Mom. Why is it you never once mentioned Libby to me? You never even introduced us. In fact, in your letters, you never ever mentioned her name."

Lenore folded her arms and sat back with a triumphant look. "We both know how you always resist my selections. I knew if I ever suggested the match, you'd automatically reject the idea. I decided to sit back and let you figure this one out for yourself."

Could this possibly be true? Greg wondered. Had his mother really had the foresight to see how perfect Libby would be for him? But he still had his doubts.

"Just think about it for a minute, Greg," his mother continued. "You know I always return to Florida in September. Why do you think I stayed in Michigan until late October this year? I nearly froze to death waiting for you to discover what was right here in front of your eyes all the time."

This brought on a spate of laughter at the head table, and others strained to hear what the joke was about.

"I can verify what she's saying," Patty chimed in. "On her way home from Michigan, she stopped in Atlanta to visit me for a few days, and she told me all about it. I just figured this was another one of Mom's attempts to get her son married; I never dreamed things would really turn out the way she planned."

"So I never had a chance, did I?" With his arm still draped over Libby's shoulders, Greg shook his head and grinned at his scheming mother. He turned to the crowd and, holding up Lenore's right hand, he proclaimed for all to hear, "Meet my mom, the world's best matchmaker." And once again, the guests clapped and cheered.

Danny, not to be outdone, demanded some of the credit for himself. "Dad's kinda slow sometimes, Grandma. That's why he needs you and me to help him work these things out. I been tryin' for weeks to tell him who we needed, and who he should pick, an' I reckon he finally got the message."

A Letter To Our Readers

Dear Reader:

In order that we might better contribute to your reading enjoyment, we would appreciate your taking a few minutes to respond to the following questions. We welcome your comments and read each form and letter we receive. When completed, please return to the following:

Rebecca Germany, Fiction Editor
Heartsong Presents
PO Box 719
Uhrichsville, Ohio 44683

1. Did you enjoy reading *Condo Mania* by Muncy G. Chapman?
   ☐ Very much! I would like to see more books
     by this author!
   ☐ Moderately. I would have enjoyed it more if

   _____

   _____

   _____

2. Are you a member of **Heartsong Presents**? Yes ☐ No ☐
   If no, where did you purchase this book?_____

   _____

3. How would you rate, on a scale from 1 (poor) to 5 (superior), the cover design?_____

4. On a scale from 1 (poor) to 10 (superior), please rate the following elements.

   _____ Heroine   _____ Plot

   _____ Hero   _____ Inspirational theme

   _____ Setting   _____ Secondary characters

5. These characters were special because_____

_____

_____

6. How has this book inspired your life?_____

_____

_____

7. What settings would you like to see covered in future
   Heartsong Presents books?_____

_____

_____

8. What are some inspirational themes you would like to see
   treated in future books?_____

_____

_____

9. Would you be interested in reading other **Heartsong
   Presents** titles?   Yes ❑   No ❑

10. Please check your age range:
    ❑ Under 18   ❑ 18-24   ❑ 25-34
    ❑ 35-45   ❑ 46-55   ❑ Over 55

11. How many hours per week do you read?_____

Name _____

Occupation _____

Address _____

City _____ State _____ Zip _____

RESCUE

*H*owever they communicate it, the friends you are about to make within this book are in peril—of body, heart, and soul. It may take a daring intervention—and some divine help—to get them out of their frightening situations.

Fasten your safety belt as you head into these four adventures. Life and love are at risk, but it's comforting to know that God, as always, is ultimately in control.

paperback, 464 pages, 5 ³⁄₁₆" x 8"

Hearts♥ng

HEARTSONG PRESENTS *TITLES AVAILABLE NOW:*

·····**Presents**·····

Great Inspirational Romance at a Great Price!

Heartsong Presents books are inspirational romances in contemporary and historical settings, designed to give you an enjoyable, spirit-lifting reading experience. You can choose wonderfully written titles from some of today's best authors like Hannah Alexander, Irene B. Brand, Yvonne Lehman, Tracie Peterson, and many others.

When ordering quantities less than twelve, above titles are $2.95 each.
Not all titles may be available at time of order.

Hearts♥ng Presents
Love Stories
Are Rated G!

That's for godly, gratifying, and of course, great! If you love a thrilling love story, but don't appreciate the sordidness of some popular paperback romances, **Heartsong Presents** is for you. In fact, **Heartsong Presents** is the *only inspirational romance book club* featuring love stories where Christian faith is the primary ingredient in a marriage relationship.

Sign up today to receive your first set of four, never before published Christian romances. Send no money now; you will receive a bill with the first shipment. You may cancel at any time without obligation, and if you aren't completely satisfied with any selection, you may return the books for an immediate refund!

Imagine. . .four new romances every four weeks—two historical, two contemporary—with men and women like you who long to meet the one God has chosen as the love of their lives. . . all for the low price of $9.97 postpaid.

To join, simply complete the coupon below and mail to the address provided. **Heartsong Presents** romances are rated G for another reason: They'll arrive *Godspeed!*